TONGUES OF JADE

LAURENCE YEP

TONGUES OF JADE

illustrated by David Wiesner

■ HarperCollins*Publishers*

To Dorothy and Raymond Ryder,
Who know a few tales themselves

Tongues of Jade
Text copyright © 1991 by Laurence Yep
Illustrations copyright © 1991 by David Wiesner
All rights reserved. No part of this book may be used or reproduced
in any manner whatsoever without written permission except in the
case of brief quotations embodied in critical articles and reviews.
Printed in the United States of America. For information address
HarperCollins Children's Books, a division of HarperCollins Publishers,
10 East 53rd Street, New York, NY 10022.
1 2 3 4 5 6 7 8 9 10
First Edition

Library of Congress Cataloging-in-Publication Data
Yep, Laurence.
    Tongues of jade / Laurence Yep ; illustrated by David Wiesner.
        p.   cm.
    Includes bibliographical references.
    Summary: A retelling of seventeen Chinese American folktales from
a variety of Chinese communities in the United States.
    ISBN 0-06-022470-3. — ISBN 0-06-022471-1 (lib. bdg.)
    1. Chinese Americans—Folklore. [1. Folklore, Chinese American.
2. Folklore—United States.] I. Wiesner, David, ill. II. Title.
PZ8.1.Y37To   1991   91-2119
398.2'089951073—dc20   CIP
                                                                      AC

Contents

INTRODUCTION

In ancient times, the Chinese covered their dead with various pieces of jade. In those days, the Chinese believed that jade had the power to preserve the body. In one of the stories in this collection, the jade covers a pair of eyes; but there were pieces cut to fit other parts of the body as well, including jade cut into the shape of a tongue with designs of cicadas carved onto the surface, because cicadas sleep within the ground for a number of years before emerging again. Such pieces of jade were placed in the mouths of the dead, perhaps in the hope that they would speak again.

Even now in Chinatown, you can buy jade with cicadas carved onto them—though the seller may not understand their former use.

Beyond that, though, every storyteller speaks with a tongue of jade, preserving an entire time period. My father would sometimes instruct me by telling a story. In the telling, he would frequently perform the dialogue for all the characters so that they came to life along with their surroundings.

In the nineteenth century, a large number of Chinese men left southern China to work here in America. Because of harsh immigration laws, it was difficult for their wives and children to join them. I think it was with a sense of irony that they called themselves "guests of the Golden Mountain"—which is what they called America. Far away from their families, they told tales not only to remind themselves of home, but to show how a wise man could survive in a strange, often hostile land.

However, by the twentieth century, a number of men had been able to bring their families over here, and there were growing numbers of children with roots sunk deep into America as well as China. Tales would have educated them about the China they had left or perhaps had never seen. More importantly, the tales would also have taught them how a true Chinese was to behave.

In the 1930's Jon Lee went into Oakland's Chinatown and gathered and translated sixty-nine stories as part of a WPA project. At a later period, Professor Wolfram Eberhard collected more stories in San Francisco's Chinatown.

We have no time machine to take us into the past, but we have the tales—thanks to Jon Lee and Wolfram Eberhard. Through the storyteller's voice, we can slip for a moment through that verbal portal into a vanished world where Chinese in America called themselves "guests of the Golden Mountain."

Roots

Most of the Chinese who came to America in the nineteenth century were of peasant stock, with dirt underneath their fingernails and strong ties to the land in China, where generations of their ancestors were buried. Once here, they provided much of the raw labor for western agriculture during the latter half of the nineteenth century. What ties did they develop to the soil of America—which they called the land of the Golden Mountain? Even though the Chinese called themselves "guests" of that Golden Mountain, they spent most of their lives here. "The Guardians" emphasizes the close bonds a Chinese farmer feels for the earth. Surely some of them must have come to feel similar links to the American fields and orchards where they worked for so many years.

1

*Moreover, America affected these guests during their stay in other ways. In "The Cure," the old man approaches the world with a sense of wonder that enables him to find a marvel that more commonsensical folk do not even see. Later, he is able to work a miracle because he has clung so persistently to that vision. There were Chinese who treated America in a similar fashion—though what they preserved and took home were not pieces of fruit but ideas, some of them technological. Among other things, the first electric power company in China was created not in the capital, Beijing, but in Canton in southern China, where many of the guests came from.**

And yet there must have been a price to pay. During their long sojourn in America, they had also acquired an American viewpoint, including ideas of democracy, in addition to their Chinese viewpoint. What had value in one system would be worthless illusion in another. This double vision was both a power and a curse from the nineteenth century on, as it was for Jade in the comical "The Green Magic"—and, more tragically, as it has been for the students in Tiananmen Square.

---

*H. Mark Lai and Philip Choy, Outlines: History of the Chinese in America *(San Francisco: Chinese American Studies Planning Group, 1973), p.132.*

The
Green
Magic

Once there were two brothers. Their family had farmed their land for generations and the older boy, Emerald, was happy to work in the mud and tend his rice plants; but he especially liked to grow peaches on his family's tree. His peaches were always the roundest and sweetest.

However, the younger boy, Jade, wanted to run away to become a magician. Everyone but his older brother thought he was crazy. "There's a green magic too. It's the magic of growing plants," Emerald said. "Why can't you be happy with that?"

"The green magic is a good magic and an old one," Jade said, "but one day you might need more magic than that."

So Emerald was sad but not surprised when Jade ran away one day.

5

In time, when their parents died, Emerald took over their farm. He had a way with the fields and the plants. No one's peaches were sweeter or vegetables leafier. As he worked among his plants, he would sometimes think of his brother and wonder what had happened to Jade.

The years went by. One summer, the rains did not fall. Despite all his skill, Emerald could not save his crops. So the next spring, he borrowed money from a rich man to buy seed. Again the rains did not come that year, and all Emerald's skill could not keep his crops from withering in the fields.

Now the rich man had plenty of money. In fact, he had paid more money for the exotic rocks in his garden than he had lent to Emerald. Even so, he insisted on being paid, and Emerald had to give him everything, fields and house and peach tree and all—though they all had been in his family for centuries.

His last act as the owner of the farm was to eat one last peach from his tree and save the seed, which he hung on a string around his neck. Then he cut down a stalk of bamboo and trimmed off the leaves. With the pole on his shoulders, he went to the great city to survive as best he could.

During the day, he managed to feed himself by carrying loads with his bamboo pole. At night, he slept in doorways or on the street with the other people.

Late one afternoon a crazy man appeared in the

street and began to spout gibberish. And since there was nothing that the city loved more than a new spectacle, a crowd soon gathered to laugh. Thinking there was something familiar about the voice, Emerald shoved his way through the crowd.

The man's hair dangled in a tangle, his robe was dirty and hung open, and he wore a little basket for a hat. Emerald, though, recognized his little brother.

"Poor, poor Jade," Emerald said. With his fingers Emerald combed the knots from Jade's hair. "Did you lose your senses searching for magic? Or did you find it and did its power destroy your mind? Come on. We're going to go home."

Jade only went on babbling as Emerald tied up his little brother's robes. Shouldering his pole and baskets, Emerald sadly led Jade into an alley away from the crowd.

As they walked, Emerald would ask Jade if he remembered this or that, but his little brother would only chatter on. Emerald could only decide sorrowfully, "Poor little brother. You've lost all your senses."

The bamboo rested on Emerald's shoulder with a basket hanging from each end. Jade pointed to one of them. "Hey, donkey," Jade said. "That basket's empty. Give me a ride."

Emerald thought it was just more craziness from his brother, so he only shook his head. "If you can fit in that basket, you're welcome to." But he set his baskets down as part of the sad joke.

"Fool, you have to balance the load." Plucking the peach pit from Emerald's neck, Jade set it in the rear basket. Then, with a smile, he stepped into the basket.

To humor his brother, Emerald started to straighten up; and to his surprise, the baskets were no heavier than before.

"Ar-r-re you a ghost?" the frightened Emerald asked.

"No," Jade said, and he did not look quite so crazy anymore. "I came to help you because the wheel turns and turns and it all comes around. Take me to the rich man."

Emerald argued with his little brother for a while, but Jade was firm. So Emerald picked his way over the poor people sleeping in the street until he came to the rich man's house.

It so happened that the rich man who now owned their farm had grown sick. He had tried every sort of cure. Priests had prayed over him. Doctors had poked and pried and poured all sorts of syrups down his throat, but he stayed as sick as ever.

At Jade's order, Emerald lowered the baskets to the ground. Getting out, Jade plucked the pit from the other basket and knocked at the gate before Emerald could stop him. When the gatekeeper opened it, Jade announced, "We're here for the party." And he shoved past the startled servant.

Now on his doctors' orders, the rich man was taking

in the fresh air and viewing the sunset from his garden pavilion. His only companion was his pet parrot with feathers as yellow bright as the sun.

Confidently Jade strutted through the wind-carved rocks that stood in the garden and around the lake like miniature mountains.

"Who are you? What do you want?" the rich man demanded.

Jade cleared his throat. "My brother and I have traveled a long way and we're hot and dusty. Maybe we could have something to eat and drink?"

The rich man stared in astonishment at this ragged beggar who would barge into his house and expect to eat with him.

By that time, Emerald had caught up with his brother. Horrified, he bowed low to the rich man. "Forgive him. He's crazy."

"Humph," Jade snorted. "If we cannot stay at your party, then we will have to make our own."

The gatekeeper had rounded up other servants to throw the two brothers out, but the rich man held up a hand. "He amuses me."

With a grin, Jade rubbed his hands around his stomach and gave a cough, and out hopped a rabbit almost as tall as the man. In the rabbit's paws were a pestle, mortar, and jars. With a bow, it began to juggle them all.

Then Jade turned to the astonished rich man. "The

sun is going to set. Since you've gotten your entertainment for free, may we have a lantern to light our party?"

However, the rich man's heart was as small and hard as a peach pit, and he refused.

"Well," Jade said, "if we can't have one of your lights, we will have to make our own." And Jade took a piece of paper from a table in the pavilion and tore it into a circle and hung it on a tree. Instantly the circle filled the garden with a light so sharp and silvery that the farmer could see every whisker and hair of Jade's head.

Jade folded his arms. "No party is complete without music. What about hiring some musicians to play a few of my favorite tunes?"

The rich man straightened his robes. "Certainly not!"

Jade sighed. "If we can't have your music, then we will have to make our own." And the magician picked up a chopstick and tossed it into the paper moon.

A lovely woman appeared in the moon and nodded a greeting. Although she was about the size of a thumb, she grew to normal height when she stepped onto the ground. Turning over the mortar, the rabbit beat out a tune with the pestle as the woman danced and sang.

When she was finished, Jade stared at the rich man. "We're all hungry. What about setting out a banquet?"

By now the rich man knew that Jade was no ordinary man. Even so, he shook his head. "What would my friends think if I ate with beggars?"

"Well"—Jade sighed elaborately—"If we can't go to the banquet, then we will have to make our own banquet."

And the rabbit took from his mouth a three-legged toad that was nearly as big as the rabbit. On the toad's back were a small metal kettle and a clay jar; and though the kettle was no bigger than a fist, the two brothers ate one rare dish after another. And though the jar was no longer than a thumb, they drank their fill.

"And now for dessert." Jade plucked the peach pit from his sleeve. Then, with stiff fingers, he poked a hole several inches deep into the soil and dropped the pit into the hole. Smoothing the dirt over the seed, he brought water from the lake in his cupped hands and poured it onto the spot.

Instantly, a sprout shot up and thickened into a stick and the stick into a pole until there was a full-size peach tree covered with leaves. Flowers blossomed in the moonlight, casting a sweet scent through the whole estate. And then the flowers fell and in a moment there were peaches dangling from the branches.

Jade shared these around, and they were so sweet and full that they all smacked their lips, even the rich man.

"And now all good parties must come to an end,"

Jade said. "And so it's time to settle your bill."

The rabbit put the toad into its mouth and the magician put the rabbit into his. And the woman in the moon became a chopstick again and the paper moon became just paper. And the tree became just an old broomstick.

At that moment, a servant ran into the garden to say that all the food and wine had disappeared from the kitchen.

The rich man pointed at Jade. "You're nothing but a common thief."

"And you, sir, are an uncommon one," Jade said. "I've taken only a few items that have been in your kitchen less than a day, but you've taken land that has been in our family for years."

The rich man glared at his frightened servants. "Throw him out." When his servants hesitated, he shouted, "Don't be scared. His magic is all illusion."

Before the servants could act, Jade had leaped next to the parrot's perch. "At least my magic does you no harm. Not like this creature."

"If you harm one feather, you'll pay with your head," the rich man warned.

"This is no parrot but a monster in disguise." And before everyone's horrified eyes, he killed it. "Even now," Jade announced, "if I let it go, it would escape."

However, the rich man refused to believe. "Seize him," he bellowed.

Now the rich man's servants had set out a charcoal brazier near the rich man so he could keep warm. Quickly, Jade held the corpse against the red charcoals. "You see? It doesn't burn."

Though little flames licked at the feathers, they did not even singe them. Surprised, the rich man waved his servants back. "What kind of monster is it?"

"I can show you its true shape with the three magic fires," Jade cautioned, "but are you sure you want to see it?"

"I want to see my tormentor, if it has been causing my illness," the rich man insisted.

As soon as Jade worked his spell, the parrot shrieked from the brazier, "Why do you persecute me, Master? What have I done to you?"

Jade looked heavenward. "Let lightning cleanse this garden of all evil."

With a scream, the parrot disappeared, leaving a hideous creature writhing in its place. Releasing it, Jade jumped back as it leaped away from the pavilion and into the air.

The next moment there was a flash of light that blinded them all. As they blinked their eyes and groped about, a thunderous boom deafened them.

When they had all recovered the use of their eyes and ears, Jade stood before the rich man. "What is your life worth? Give my brother back his land," Jade said, "and give him money for seed."

And the trembling rich man gave the deed to the land and a basket of silver to the astonished Emerald.

When they were outside the mansion again, Emerald wanted his younger brother to return to the farm with him, but Jade would not go.

"We have two kinds of magic," Jade said. "You create life while I create illusions. You can practice your art in a small patch of dirt, but I must have the whole earth for mine."

And so Jade left Emerald; but every year when the peaches had ripened to a sweet fullness, Emerald would announce to the air, "It's time now."

And a dozen peaches would disappear from the tree. And Emerald would know that somewhere in the world his brother was enjoying his green magic.

The
Guardians

There was once a boy who, when he was old enough, helped his father in the fields. From sunrise to sunset, he helped with the hoeing and the weeding, moving down the rows of the rice plants, tugging his feet out of the mud at every step. Or he would help his father fertilize the fields with a long-handled dipper, wrinkling his nose at the smell, for the fertilizer was made from human and animal dung. At times his stomach and leg muscles would hurt from bending over so much.

Sometimes, the sun beat down on him even through his big straw hat and he would start to sweat. Then dust and burrs from the weeds would cling to his skin. The boy would try to wipe them off; but his father would keep on working down the rows of plants as if his skin were like leather. Right away the boy would feel guilty and hurry to catch up with his father.

One day it began to rain, and the wind whipped the raindrops into the boy's face so hard that they stung like needles. Immediately he stopped and tried to hide his face in his arms. As playfully as a cat with a mouse, the wind instantly sent the rain slashing at his back instead. His father, though, went on working just as steadily as before.

The boy put up with the hard work and the long hours because his father and all the other farmers did; but one day, as he worked in the muddy field, he pulled a leg free and saw ugly leeches sucking at his ankle. With a cry, he pulled them off and flung them away. There were ugly little round wounds on his leg now, and they stung when he set his foot back in the mud. That was simply too much.

The boy stopped and began to cry. "How can you stand it?" he asked his father.

His father straightened up slowly and looked at the boy sadly. "A farmer's life is hard; but it feeds us—even if barely."

And the boy felt so ashamed that he stopped crying and went back to work. That evening as he limped home with a sore back and legs, the boy stopped with his father at two small statues. The wind and rain had worn the statues down so much that they looked more like the nearby stones than like statues.

His father squatted down ponderously, as if his legs and knees were as sore as the boy's. With one gnarled thumb, the father tried to rub some of the dirt from the statues' faces, but their features were no clearer.

"Do you know who they are, boy?"

The boy had seen them all his life but had never given them a thought. "No."

"This is the earth god and his wife. Once they were farmers just like us, but in their time, farmers had to break up the dirt with their bare hands. Farming was so hard that they could not grow much food. And they were even more tired than you are, because they had so much extra work to do.

"So one day the villagers gathered together to talk over what they could do. They spent most of their time complaining to one another. 'Our children are starving,' they said to one another.

"Then one old farmer spoke up. 'We have to do something. Let's ask Heaven for help.'

"Everyone agreed that it was such a good idea that he was elected on the spot to speak to Heaven. So the messenger went up—don't ask me how.

"The first creatures he met up there were huge—with four hoofed legs and black hides and horns. They were so strange that the messenger was afraid. 'Don't hurt me,' he begged.

"But the creatures were the first buffalo. They just laughed. 'And what are you, you puny thing?'

"'I am a human,' the old farmer said, and chatted with them a bit, for they were just as friendly as they were big. So finally he said, 'You're so big and strong. Won't you help us?'

"The buffalo were willing, but the gods would not let them go because Heaven was afraid that humans would mistreat them.

"The messenger promised that they would be safe and offered himself as their guarantee. The buffalo were sent with the messenger and helped clear more land and break up more soil than ever before. The plants, though, took time to grow, and one villager became afraid that his family would starve in the meantime. So one night he killed the buffalo and ate them.

"Naturally Heaven was so furious that everyone expected some terrible revenge. However, the messenger went up again and offered himself. 'Punish me. It is my fault for not guarding the buffalo as I should have.'

"And his wife, who loved him, stepped forward and asked to be with her husband no matter what the punishment might be.

"And so Heaven ordered that when they died, they would live in the open forever, where they would suffer from the wind and the rain, the sun and the cold."

After hearing the story, the boy felt sorry for the little earth gods. At least he had a house to go to at night. That evening, by the moonlight, he wove some bits of straw into two small hats. The next morning, he hid them in his sleeve as he and his father ate a breakfast of cold rice and tea. Then they walked down the winding path that led from their village on the side of the ridge down to the fields below. The boy, though, lagged behind his father and stopped by the little earth gods.

"It's not fair that you don't have some protection," the boy said, and he tied the two hats to the statues' heads.

Feeling much better, the boy went down to the fields. That day, when the rain shower fell and later when the sun beat down hot and heavy, the boy smiled to himself because the two statues at least had the same protection as he.

That evening as they left the fields, the father noticed the two hats on the statues, and when he saw his son smiling, he understood what had happened. Though the boy tried to protest, his father took the hats from the statues and crumpled them up in his fist. "What Heaven has ordered we must obey." He sighed.

Months later, the boy was hurrying home one evening. He had been weeding a field by himself and had lost track of the time. Suddenly a wind swirled around him like a giant invisible bird. Shivering in the unexpected chill, the boy tried to pick up his pace, but the wind snatched him up. The boy gasped as if giant icy claws had closed around his chest and swept him forward faster than before. He hardly had to move his legs at all.

It was as if the wind itself were alive. "Beware! Beware!" a voice wailed in his ear.

There was a blinding flash of light, and the wind vanished as abruptly as it had come. The boy fell to his knees, blinking his eyes in darkness that seemed even deeper than before.

While other people would have been blind in that blackness, the boy was still able to see because his mother fed her family meals to strengthen their eyes. Some gossips said she even fed them cats' eyes so that they could see like cats at night; however, most people didn't believe that story because the mother was a kindly sort of woman.

Whatever she fed her family, it worked. As the boy knelt there, looking all around, he thought he saw part of the darkness split away and form the silhouette of a long-limbed man—like the shadow of a person at sunset when the shadows can stretch clear across a field.

Bouncing on its thin, long legs, the shadow began to stalk toward him. Springing to his feet, the boy flung himself in the opposite direction. He stumbled down a dike and plunged into the field, where the mud clung and sucked at his arms and legs as he got to his feet. Trying to run through the mud was like trying to race through glue.

Because he could feel an iciness at the back of his neck, he knew the shadow was gaining. With a lurch, he struggled up the side of a dike and back onto the path, where he darted away.

Above him, on the side of the ridge, he could see the lights of the village gleaming; but the shadow was even closer now. He could feel icy claws nipping at his back. Staring up longingly at the village, the boy knew he would never make it.

Suddenly his foot caught on a rock and he fell down hard upon the rocky dirt. Instantly, he rolled to his right and felt a cold iciness where he had been—as if the shadow had pounced upon that spot. He sat up, expecting those icy claws to sink into him. Instead, he saw a man and a woman rise from the rocks. They were not flesh and blood, though, but transparent—as if they had been cut out of rice paper.

Through their translucent bodies, the boy could see the shadow charge toward him and he cringed, waiting to die. However, as thin and fragile as they seemed, they caused the shadow to smash to a halt against them. Hovering, the shadow seemed shapeless for a moment; then it grew more arms than an octopus and at the end of each tentacle was a claw. Furious, it sliced at the man and woman, but without any effect, and then shoved and lunged at them. Still sitting, the frightened boy slid back a yard, but the shadow could not reach him through the pair. Though the shadow thrust at the shapes angrily, it could not break through them to get to the boy. With one last frustrated swipe of its claws, it howled through a dozen mouths,

"Lucky, lucky, lucky."

Then the shadow plunged back into the night.

As the boy sat there, not quite believing he was still alive, the man and woman shrank, sliding back into the ground. He was still sitting there when his father found him.

By the lantern in his father's hand, the boy saw that he had fallen on the rocks near the little roofless shrine of the earth gods. When his father helped him home, the boy told everyone what had happened. His mother instantly understood. "It was the two earth gods who saved you. Tomorrow we'll go burn incense to them."

The next morning, though, the boy was too sick to go with his mother. When she caressed his head, his hair came out in great clumps—much to his parents' alarm. "The monster has done this," the mother decided.

Leaving her husband to tend the boy, the mother hurried down by herself to the statues. Bowing respectfully to them, the mother lit slender sticks of incense and stuck them into the dirt before the statues.

Every day the boy was sick, his mother burned incense to the earth gods. It was the very first thing she did each morning. In time, the boy's hair started to grow back and he began to feel stronger.

When the boy finally recovered, he joined his father back in the fields. But every morning that he passed by the earth gods, he would stop and kneel. Bowing to them, he would promise, "You saved my life. I won't forget you." And, lighting a stick of incense, he would thrust it in front of the two earth gods who had not forgotten his small act of kindness.

The
Cure

Once a boy went up a hillside to gather wood and grass for the stove, when he heard a woman speak from a nearby bush. Though low, her words rang as sharp and clear as crystal.

"If I have to sit cooped up inside here one more moment, I will simply die," she said.

"It's so frightfully boring," echoed a second.

"Now, now, my dears. Good things come to those who wait," a third woman answered.

However, when the curious boy parted the leaves of the bush, he saw only a winter melon. Oval in shape, it was colored a whitish green and looked as if it had been carved from jade.

Straightening up, he called to the women that they had forgotten their melon; but when there was no answer, he looked inside the bush again. "I wonder if it's good to eat."

Just as his hands reached out to take it, a woman declared sharply, "Do we make a habit of eating your roof?"

"No snacking allowed," scolded a second.

A third declared firmly, "And wipe off any finger-prints."

Snatching back his hands, the boy squatted down. "Who are you?" he asked. "What are you doing inside there?"

When no one answered from within the melon, he knocked at the top. "Is anyone home?"

"Stop that," the three women chorused.

"Do we make a thunderstorm in your home?" one of them demanded. "Don't be rude."

After that, the boy left them alone; but each day, when he was finished with his chores, he would go up to the hillside, part the bush, and examine the magical melon. Each day, it was larger than the day before. He even began to think of the melon as his own because it was his own private secret.

He watered it and tended it, and though the women never spoke to him again—not even to say thank you—he could hear them speaking to one another, and he would sit and listen. Sometimes they spoke wist-fully of their former lives in a faraway palace where the flowers of the garden were all of gold and jade and other precious stones. However, as punishment for some crime they had committed, they had been reborn inside the melon.

Feeling sorry for them, the boy tended the melon until it finally grew so large that it stuck out of the bush.

Of course, the other villagers were bound to notice it. Word of the marvel soon spread and a crowd soon gathered to wonder at the miraculous melon.

Finally, a tall man shoved his way rudely through the crowd. He was one of those big-stick bullies who liked to mind everyone else's business but his own. He was good with his fists and feet, so he liked nothing better than to pick a fight. He didn't care how he looked. His hair was always in a tangle, and his shirt and pants were always dirty.

The bully swaggered right up to the melon. Rapping at it with his knuckles, he squeezed the top. "This melon is ripe. It ought to feed a family for a month."

"No," the boy protested as he ran up the hill. "It's mine. I saw it first."

"So you weren't going to share." The bully cuffed the boy and sent him rolling into the others. "Just for that, you won't get any."

The boy sat up in time to see the bully shake the melon, trying to break the stem from the vine. "Tell him not to," he said to the women in the melon.

The others thought the boy was speaking to them. "If we try to tell him that, we'll get the same thing you did."

"Tell him, tell him," the boy said.

The bully suddenly gave a roar and whirled around. "Which one of you called me Fatty?" He pointed at a woman. "Was it you?"

The woman hid behind her husband. As her terrified husband began to shake, the woman said, "It was someone else."

The bully strode back toward the other villagers. "No one insults me."

The boy picked up a rock and ran between the bully and the melon.

"Nobody from the village insulted you—though they'd like to. It was the women in the melon."

The bully turned around and stared at the boy. "The boy's touched."

"And you've got the manners of a pig," said a voice from the melon.

"So you do tricks with your voice," the bully grunted. "Touched or not, no one talks to me like that."

He charged toward the boy. The boy got ready to throw the rock at the bully when suddenly there was a blinding flash—as if lightning had hit the hillside.

The bully threw himself down with a cry, and it was a moment before the boy could see again. When he could, he saw the villagers all pointing behind him with their mouths hanging open. Turning around, he saw that the melon had split open. Light spilled out of the crack and then was hidden by the silhouette of a tiny woman. She was no taller than the boy's forearm, and she was absolutely beautiful.

"Such manners," the woman said. She stepped out. Dressed in an antique gown of red, she had roses ornamenting her hair.

A second woman, identical to the first except that she wore purple and lilies decorated her hair, followed her. "You really can't expect much."

"Are they trying to catch flies?" asked the third as she stepped out. She wore yellow and there were poppies in her hair.

The boy knelt and bowed his head to the three women. He knew they must be some sort of spirits. "Since your home has a hole in it, would you like to come to mine?"

The first looked up at the sky. "It does look like rain."

"It won't be long now, anyway," said the second.

"He still might have had some consideration." The third glared at the bully.

For once the bully had an opponent against whom his fists and feet were useless. When he opened his mouth to explain, just a squeak came out. The three spirits smiled. "At least we don't have to listen to him."

And though the bully went red in the face trying to shout, he could only make small, mouse-like noises.

Hurriedly the boy borrowed a basket, and the three

women climbed into it and were carried down to the village.

The boy was afraid of what they would think of his family's house, but the first spirit merely sniffed. "It's not as bad as it could be, my dears."

Though the spirits lived within his house, they ate and drank nothing and talked only among themselves, but on the tenth day, the first spirit spoke to the boy. "Let me express our gratitude for your many kindnesses."

"You have made a hard exile a little easier," explained the second.

The third smiled at the boy. "Remember: Good things come to those who wait."

And no sooner had she uttered those words than the three spirits died—or, rather, passed on. Their small bodies fell to the ground, but their souls returned to whatever place was their home. When the boy tried to gather up the bodies, they turned to dust in his hands.

The boy went up to see the melon. It had shrunk so that it was the original size it was when he had first seen it, but the pieces had not dried or rotted away. Instead, they looked as fresh as when the melon had burst. Though it looked like an ordinary enough melon now, the boy picked up the pieces as souvenirs and brought them home.

Time went on, and the bully got back his voice. I

would like to say that the spirits' punishment made him a better person, but the bully just wasn't the sort to learn new tricks. He remained just as quarrelsome as ever, but all anyone had to do was mention the word "melon" and his voice would crack—much to his embarrassment.

When the boy had grown into a man and married and begun to raise a family, he made a point of planting roses, lilies, and poppies in the little courtyard of his house. As is the way of the world, people began to forget about the spirit-women, and they teased him about wasting his time on flowers when he should be tending his fields.

As the years went by, everyone passed on who had seen the spirits, except for the boy, who was now an old man. "Once," he tried to tell the younger villagers, "there was a wonder that passed through our village, three little spirits as lovely as spring. They came from inside a magical melon."

He tried to show them what had once been the magical melon. "And here it is. In all this time, the melon hasn't rotted or changed since I took it from its vine."

The other villagers, including his own son, laughed at him. "That old thing! You just chopped up a melon right now to fool us. Go and play your pranks on somebody else."

Eventually, the old man found himself wishing that someone from the old days, even the bully, were alive, but there was only himself. Only his grandson believed in him and asked to hear about the magical melon.

There came a terrible time when a plague spread through the district and the demons of the underworld took whomever they wanted—rich and poor, young and old, beautiful and ugly. All were their victims. The priests couldn't pray it away and the doctors couldn't doctor it away. Nothing worked.

And then the old man's grandson took sick. The fever burned inside the little body. The old man sat with him day and night, putting wet rags on his grandson's forehead. And he watched the little body waste away. It didn't seem very long before the demons of the underworld would come to claim him with all the other victims.

His son patted the old man on the back. "Rest, or the demons will take you too."

"I wish they would. I've outlived everything, even the magic." Wearily, the old man left his son to tend the boy. However, the old man did not lie down. Instead, he went outside and asked everyone he met what remedies they would recommend, but they all suggested things he had already tried.

Discouraged, he returned to his home to find an old beggar sitting just within his gate. Instead of turning the beggar out, he asked him desperately, "Can you think of something to help my grandson?"

The beggar leaned on his crutch and pursed his lips in thought. Then he nodded. "You might try making a soup out of that melon of yours." The voice was clear, like a bell, and the old man immediately knew it was one of the spirits in disguise.

He knelt and bowed his head. "Thank you," he said, but when he looked up, the beggar had vanished, and where the beggar had been was a bright red rose.

He went back inside and tore the house apart until he found the box containing the fragments of winter melon. Cutting a piece from one slice, he dropped it into boiling water. When the soup was ready, he poured it into a bowl and brought it to his grandson. His grandson was too sick to even sit up and eat, so the old man had his son hold the boy up while the old man spooned the soup between the child's lips.

By that evening the boy was eating solid food, and by the next morning he was walking about. When the other villagers saw that his grandson was cured, they begged the old man for some of the very same melon that they had once mocked.

The kindly old man could not hold a grudge against his neighbors and kin, so he gave slices of melon to whoever asked. In that way, the plague and the demons of the underworld were banished from the village. And after that, whenever people took sick in the village, the old man cured them with a bit of the magical melon.

As the spirits had predicted, good things came to him who waited.

Family Ties

Many of the men who came to work in America spent most of their lives apart from their families. They worked long hours here—sometimes under hostile conditions—and sent a large part of their wages back home. A strong sense of duty made them sacrifice most of their lives here.

Many of the folktales reinforce those feelings of responsibility. Though a Chinese peacock can be as vain as his western counterpart, in "Royal Robes" it is the peacock's prompt performance of his duty that brings about his initial reward of beauty.

One of the stories deals with those who refuse to follow their traditional obligations. According to Chinese custom, a bride must treat her mother-in-law as her mother, and a husband *is supposed to side with his mother rather than with his wife. As a result, an abusive mother-in-law could sometimes drive a young bride to suicide. However, in southern China, from which many husbands had gone overseas to America, the opposite case was also possible: What happens when the husband is gone and a younger, stronger woman is left with a weaker, older one? "Fish Heads" deals with just such a situation.*

Some of the families lived quite well on the money sent home by the guests in America. Reality would set in when it was the sons' turn to come to America to work. Suddenly, these boys who had lived like princes would find themselves on the bottom of the American social scale. The lessons in "The Little Emperor" would have special meaning for the sons of guests who were destined for the Golden Mountain.

Finally, I think of "The Phantom Heart" as a kind of parable for a homecoming. At best, many of the guests would have depended upon letters to communicate with their families. In some cases, this tenuous link might last ten, twenty years. What was it like for these emotional strangers to return home after so many years? What was it like to leave a bride of sixteen and come back to a wife of thirty-six? Even five years of separation can create an emotional distance between a husband and wife. In some cases, it must have taken all of the wife's patience, strength, and resourcefulness to transplant a phantom heart into a returned guest.

The
Little
Emperor

Once there was a boy whose mother spoiled him. He had been born late in her life, so she thought of him as her special child. She petted and praised him so much that the rest of the village made fun of her. "Put him in your mouth. He might melt if it rains." In fact, she spoiled her son so thoroughly that the village called him the little emperor.

Moreover, his grandfather had been a great scholar, and everyone in the village said the boy looked just like that important man. So his mother believed her son would also do well in the government exams and take a high post in the government.

Though they did not have very much, she made sacrifices to send him to school. To be honest, though, the little emperor didn't like to study; however, when he failed at his lessons, the mother blamed it on his teacher rather than on her son.

When the father died, the mother and son had to sell almost everything and take land that no one else wanted. Because the fields were so far away from the village, the little emperor had to get up before dawn and limp home after dark, where he would lie groaning from all his sore muscles. And his hands, once used to holding brush and book, were cut and calloused from field work.

"The soil is so poor and rocky that it doesn't want to grow anything," he complained to his friends. "I'm being held to the grindstone until I wear away."

The little emperor began to blame his mother for his difficult life. Though his mother worked just as hard at home, he always found fault with her. When he came home, he would look around the little shack, which was as neat as any other house in the village. "Look at this pigsty," he scolded her. "When I'm in the fields all day, what do you do—gossip? You could at least clean up a little."

The mother would bite her tongue and remind herself that her son had to grow up faster than the other boys. Feeling guilty, she would swallow her angry words and get the broom to sweep a floor she had already swept that day.

Because the fields were so far away from the village, she used to bring his supper to the little emperor. His mother, though, was not a young woman, and the dis-

tance from their house to the fields was really too great
for her.

One afternoon when she was late bringing his meal
of rice, he hit her. Since his hands were browned by
the sun and roughened by field work, they were as
hard as leather-wrapped rocks and really hurt. "You
lazy old woman. How do you expect me to work in the
fields all day with nothing in my belly?" And he
slapped her again.

The mother said nothing. She did not even raise her
hands to protect herself. A couple of neighbors happened to be working in a nearby field. They now felt
sorry for the woman they had once teased. "Don't be
disrespectful to your mother," they scolded him.

Immediately the woman turned to defend her son.
"He's just tired and frustrated from working all day.
Aren't you?" And she left them shaking their heads
and muttering.

That evening when the little emperor returned to
the village, people gave him funny looks. She was
afraid to say anything when I was around, he complained to himself, but as soon as she was out of my
sight, she couldn't wait to turn the whole village
against me. That made him even angrier, so he began
to slap his mother at every excuse.

One day, it had been especially hot, and the little
emperor felt as if he were trying to work inside a fur-
nace. Every breath hurt his lungs, and his clothes were

drenched with sweat. It was so hot that the other farmers quit working the fields; but the boy was determined to go on. When he saw the others trudging away, already exhausted, their hoes resting on their shoulders, he felt like going too. However, he forced himself to stay. "The only way we will climb out of our poverty," he said to himself, "is if I don't baby myself. I have to keep on working."

One more row, he would tell himself as the sweat stung his eyes, one more row and then I can think about quitting. And when the row was done, he would start over again. Satisfied with his efforts, he congratulated himself. He could measure the time by his shadow on the ground. "I'll take a rest when my mother comes with my supper. I'll have earned it then."

The heat, though, made it even more of an effort for his mother to deliver the little emperor's dinner. She could take only small, unsteady steps as she gasped in the hot air.

As a result, she took even longer than usual. Her son had kept his word not to stop until his mother came, but he resented that he had been made to work even longer than normal. A slave would get treated better than I do, he said to himself angrily.

When he saw the familiar figure of his mother shuffling toward him, it seemed to him as if she were strolling along, and that made him even more angry.

"What kept you?" he shouted. "Do I have to starve every day?"

The mother panted as she tried to explain. "I'm not as young as I used to be, and my legs are not young and strong like yours. It takes me longer to walk that distance."

The boy was in a rage now. "Then set out earlier."

"I have my own chores to do," the mother said.

"Liar! You expect me to slave away all day while you sit up in the house gossiping with the neighbors." Raising his hoe, he swung it so that the shaft thumped against his mother's back.

Though she had put up with the slaps patiently, this was simply too much. Shocked, his mother stumbled across the fields back toward the village. "You can run fast enough now," her son bellowed.

Once she was safely in the village, the weeping woman went to a neighbor's house and stayed there. Her friends wanted to gather the other neighbors and speak to her son that very night about his awful behavior, but the woman refused, insisting that there were always two sides to every quarrel.

The next day, the little emperor was back in the fields when he heard loud cheeping. Craning back his head, he saw a nest high up in a tree where a small bird was feeding her babies. As the young birds opened their beaks and chirped demandingly, the mother bird gave a worm to each.

As the little emperor watched the mother tend to her children lovingly, he began to remember how his own mother had cared for him. She had put up with all sorts of hardships to raise him, and now, when others her age were turning the chores over to someone else, she was still trying to do her work as always.

As he stared up at the birds with their gaping beaks and insistent calls, he thought, I've been just as ugly as those things. And thinking of how patient his mother had been, the little emperor broke into tears. "How could I be such a monster? Even if I weren't her son, I've been unfair. When my mother comes with my rice, I'll ask her to forgive me." And weeping, he went back to work.

In the meantime, his mother had gathered up her courage and returned to the shack to cook her son's supper. Though she set out early for the fields, her old legs just could not carry her and she had to rest frequently. As a result, the old woman was late again.

When the little emperor saw his mother hobbling along with bowls of rice and hot vegetables, he began to run to her. In his eagerness to apologize, though, he forgot that he was still carrying the hoe in his hand.

Now the old woman's eyesight was none too good, so she did not see his cheerful expression. She could, however, make out the hoe in his hand. Scared that he was going to beat her again, she flung the bowls down and turned to run. However, she tripped in one of the furrows and hit her head against a rock.

The little emperor fell to his knees beside his mother and tried to wake her, and when he realized she was dead, he began to cry. "You died because I was someone you were afraid of. Now it's time for me to become someone worthy of you."

He knelt there weeping through the night, stopping, exhausted, only as the sun rose. At first, the neighbors thought the little emperor had killed his mother, but his eyes were black and blue from crying—some even claimed to have seen drops of blood rather than tears fall from his eyes. His sorrow was so deep, they decided that it must have been an accident as he claimed.

After that, though, the little emperor was a different person. There was not one day he did not weep with shame. There was not one day during the rest of his life that he did not stop at her grave. In all that time, too, he did not take off his white robe of mourning, which over the years became spotted from his tears. When he finally died, people said he had simply wept himself to death.

Some people had the idea of building a temple. When it was done, they put his robe inside in a special place. The temple and the little emperor's robe became quite famous—especially among exasperated parents who would tell their children to give them respect before it was too late.

Royal
Robes

Long, long ago, peacocks and crabs did not look as they do now. The first peacock had only plain brown feathers; and though the first crab had eight legs, he was quite round and quite tall.

In those days, the peacock was as vain as he was dull, so he often served as the butt of the crab's jokes, for the crab liked to speak his own mind, not caring whose feelings he hurt.

In fact, the crab had insulted the peacock so many times that the bird would leave as soon as he saw the creature striding toward him.

One day the crab finally called to the peacock, "Wait. Where are you going?"

The peacock turned cautiously. "I'm leaving before you can make fun of me again."

Seeing a chance to play his greatest prank of all, the

crab cocked his head to one side. "The timbre. The tone. Why haven't I noticed how beautiful your voice is?"

"It is?" the peacock asked suspiciously.

"You know how blunt I am," the crab said. "Well, I've never heard anything more exquisite. Please sing for me."

In fact, the peacock was tone-deaf, so when he tried to sing, the words came out in a screech, but the crab pretended to faint in ecstasy at the loveliness of the peacock's voice.

"Oh dear, oh dear. What have I done?" the peacock said as he fanned the crab with a wing.

After a moment, the crab pretended to wake up again and said, "You sing more beautifully than the nightingale."

The peacock was puzzled. "That's not what the other birds say."

"That's because they're jealous," the crab insisted.

And the peacock believed the crab because he wanted to. "I bet it was the nightingale himself who put them up to it."

The crab tapped his shell thoughtfully. "You'll show them. You can entertain the king."

The peacock looked self-consciously at his drab plumage. "I couldn't."

"What a selfish beast you are," the crab snapped. "Isn't the king kind? Doesn't he see that you're safe and always have enough to eat?"

The peacock hung his head in shame as he had to admit that the crab was right.

"Then," the crab argued, "if his subjects can lighten his burden, they should."

Bit by bit, the crab convinced the reluctant bird that it was his patriotic duty to amuse their ruler.

Leaving the peacock to practice, the crab went to the palace to arrange the royal concert. Then he hurried back to flatter the peacock as the bird rehearsed his tunes. So clever was the crab that by the appointed day the peacock believed he was a great musician.

The peacock strutted proudly into the palace, but when he saw the king and his court in all their finery, he almost lost his nerve. There were parrots with their rainbow feathers and monkeys in their bright golden fur. The humans wore colorful embroidered robes of silk and satin, but the finest robe of all was the king's, with metallic blues and greens and golds. Compared to them, the peacock with his brown feathers seemed very drab and ordinary indeed.

"Maybe I should borrow a scarf or something," the peacock suggested in a low voice to the crab.

"When they hear your voice," the crab urged, "they won't care how you look."

So the peacock walked on. Behind him, the crab began to imitate his victim by kicking out all eight legs, left, right, left, right. When the king and his court began to laugh, the peacock was confused. When he turned, the crab stopped and pretended to be studying a gold-covered column. "Lovely work, isn't it?" the crab asked.

"Um, yes," the peacock murmured. Turning around, he began to parade solemnly along. Once again, the crab began to swagger, and all the humans and animals couldn't help laughing.

Again the peacock whirled around, but the crab was too quick. He stopped strutting and simply stood there looking up at the roof beams. "How high do you think it is?" he asked pleasantly.

The peacock glared at the crab but reminded himself that he must be dignified in front of the king. "I don't know," he had to admit.

Looking grave and thoughtful, the bird stopped before the throne and bowed low. There was another laugh as the crab copied the bird with exaggerated motions and gestures.

Still puzzled, the plain bird straightened up and repeated the speech that the crab had written for him. "Your Highness, in gratitude for your many kindnesses to all of us animals, I would like to present this little entertainment."

With a smile, the king raised a hand. "We thank you for your kindness." He used the imperial "we" when he meant "I."

With another little bow, the peacock began. Looks

and smiles were exchanged during the first song. By the second, people and animals began to giggle. During the third, they began to laugh openly. Humans guffawed. Horses whinnied. Cows mooed.

When the peacock stopped, the crab kept urging him to go on. "Sing, sing. For heaven's sake, sing," he hissed. "You're doing splendidly."

"They're laughing at a sad song," the peacock whispered back to the crab.

"They're laughing because the nightingale and the minstrel are so jealous, they have the funniest expressions on their faces. Sing."

So the peacock finished the song; but before he could begin a fourth, the king held up his hands. "Enough. We'd rather hear knives sharpened."

Horrified, the peacock turned on the crab. "You tricked me."

The crab shrugged massively. "The important thing was to entertain the king, and we have."

"And it is much appreciated," the king agreed. "We haven't had such a good laugh in a long time."

Now that his prank was over, the crab could be his usual rude self. "Can you imagine the nerve of that thing?" And the crab laughed the loudest of anyone.

Embarrassed, the poor peacock hung his head and slunk out of the palace.

In no time, the crab had spread news of the practical joke throughout the kingdom, and the poor bird had become so ashamed and frightened that he hid himself from everyone. "I will never, ever, go out again," he said.

Not long after that, though, the king grew quite ill. He called in his parrot messengers. "Tell our people that we are sick."

Immediately, the parrots flew from the palace, cawing, "The king is sick. The king is sick." They flew over the towns and farms and over the mountains and jungles.

Now for all of his vanity, the peacock truly loved his king; so when he heard the announcement deep within his hiding place, he forgot all about his vow. "They say laughter cures many ills. If it would help the king, I would even sing for him again."

And so he went rushing out of his hiding place, not caring who saw him and who might laugh. His wings were too short to let him fly for long, so he flew and then ran, hopped and then flew again.

Being a natural gossip, the crab was one of the first creatures to hear the news; and though he also felt sorry for the king, he couldn't help chatting about it with the first creature he bumped into. "What do you think is wrong?" he asked the monkey when he told him the news.

"I don't know." The monkey shook his head anxiously. "But I'm going to see." And he began to swing through the trees.

"What if the king's disease is contagious?" the crab wondered out loud, but the monkey had already disappeared among the trees.

All that day, the crab wandered through the jungle discussing the terrible news with whatever animal he met, until he couldn't find anyone else. "Humph, they must all be at the palace," the crab said, and so he finally loped toward there as well.

Everyone in the kingdom had hurried to the palace to see how their beloved king was, but the peacock, who had been the most worried, had been first. Wings and feet aching, and puffing with the effort, the brown bird staggered into the palace. "What. . . may I do . . . for the king?" he panted.

The cow dipped her head and made a mark on a long list. "We are doing everything we can for the king. Would you please wait?"

The peacock looked around the magnificent courtroom and remembered his earlier humiliation here. "I would rather not."

"The king has commanded that all who come must stay here," the cow informed him.

"Then I can only do what he wishes." The peacock bowed solemnly, but he found a quiet little place behind some big vases and hid there.

As each human and animal came to the palace, the cow also requested him or her to remain. Then the cow crossed off their names on a long list. Finally, the crab trotted through the doors.

"So this is where everybody is," he said. "What's the news?"

However, no one knew any more than before; but as soon as the crab entered the courtroom, the cow made a last mark on the list and ordered the doors to be shut. Then another servant rolled up the list and followed the cow as she hurried away.

A moment later, she returned, bellowing, "All bow, all bow before His Highness."

Six servants entered the courtroom, and on their shoulders was a litter carved out of wood with dragons and other royal animals. The carvings were coated with gold and the rest of the wood was lacquered a bright red. And on the litter was the king himself, though he could barely sit up in the chair. He was dressed in his most beautiful robe of blue and green, which glittered as he was carried along.

"All bow, all bow," the cow commanded.

Everyone, both human and beast, bowed low before the king who had ruled so wisely. And in his hiding place, the peacock lowered his head as he wept for his ailing ruler.

Though the servants set the litter down beside the throne, the king was not strong enough even to walk that far, so he had to be carried there. When he spoke, he could barely whisper, but it was so hushed in the courtroom and it had been designed so well that everyone could hear his words.

The king, barely able to see, looked around the courtroom sadly. "Our good people, we are near death and must leave you soon."

His subjects in the courtroom begged him not to leave them alone, and the king smiled weakly.

"It is not our will either, but it must be so. However, as we once took care of all creatures, we were curious who would take care of us." His head nodding with illness, he turned to the servant with the list. "Who was the first?"

The cow consulted the list, which another servant held up for her, and then bowed to the king. "The peacock, Your Highness."

"Bring the peacock to us," the king commanded.

At first, they couldn't find the trembling peacock, who was crouched down behind the vases, but eventually the cow found him and dragged the embarrassed bird before the king.

"I didn't mean any harm," the peacock pleaded.

The king smiled at the plain, brown bird. "And you have done none. You were first, and for that we are grateful, for you must love us very much." He looked around the courtroom. "Receive our own royal robe and wear it as a sign of our love." He leaned forward so the servants could take his robe and drape it around the peacock, who finally had something to be proud of.

Then the king turned to the cow once more. "And who was the last?"

The cow checked the list again. "The crab, Your Highness."

"Let the crab come to us," he ordered.

When the crab was brought before the throne, the king frowned. "How dare you?" the king demanded. "We have done so much for you, and yet you care nothing for us, or you would not have been last."

The crab gulped and without thinking spoke bluntly. "Someone had to be last, Your Highness."

The king was angry at the crab's rudeness and turned to his servant. "We have tried to be kind, but if there is one thing we cannot stand, it is ingratitude. Let this beast's back and legs be broken at once."

"This is all your fault," the crab snapped at the cow. "You should have warned me, you old leather bag."

The crab had insulted one too many creatures. Angrily, the cow brought down a hoof and smashed him flat. Ashamed, the crab scuttled away.

Shortly after that, the king died.

And that is why peacocks have such lovely feathers and are symbols of dignity and beauty, while crabs are flat and must creep forever in the mud.

Fish
Heads

Once a man had to go away on a trip, leaving his wife and mother alone at home. The mother was old and her eyes were going bad, so she found it hard to work. Now the daughter-in-law, Dove, had quite a temper, and she thought her mother-in-law was lying. "You get away with murder when your son's here, but he's gone now."

So Dove ordered the old woman to sweep up the house while she shopped for their supper. Outside, the young woman met an old fisherman in a tattered straw hat, his wet pants clinging to his calves. "How about a fine, fat trout, lady?" He held up a fish on a line.

"I've seen twigs that were thicker." Dove snorted. "I'll give you two cash for it." Cash were round coins with square holes.

Now the fish was worth far more than that, but

Dove would not budge from her first price. Finally the old fisherman gave her a sour grin. "Our actions shape us, lady." But he held out his palm for the two coins.

When Dove returned, she found her mother-in-law sweeping up a small storm of dust. Satisfied that she was finally setting the house in order, Dove cleaned and gutted the fish and then cooked it. When supper was ready, she went to inspect her mother-in-law's handiwork and found that the nearsighted old woman had brushed all the dust onto her daughter-in-law's sleeping mat.

Dove was furious. "I'm not some mouse who can be bullied by a mother-in-law. You did that on purpose so you can get out of your chores."

The old woman insisted that her eyes were truly bad, but Dove refused to believe her. Their neighbors, hearing Dove, had gathered outside.

"Shame on you," they said to Dove. "You're supposed to treat your mother-in-law like your own mother."

"None of your business," Dove snapped. "She might fool hicks like you, but not me." And she began to turn her tongue and her imagination upon the neighbors as well.

The old woman, who hated offending anyone, apologized right away and asked everyone to leave. When they were alone, the old woman smiled. "I'll try to help. Let me make dinner."

"While you were playing your pranks, I steamed a fish in black bean sauce," the daughter-in-law said slyly.

The old woman eased herself down on the stool where she always sat, and Dove set a bowl of rice in front of her. "So that was what that good smell was."

"The fish is awful scrawny and bony, though," Dove said. "Here. Since your eyes are so bad, I'll divide it in half and put your portion on top of your rice."

The old woman was pleased by the kindness, but it was really a test. Dove gave the old woman the fish head and kept the rest of the fish for herself. She's bound to complain that I've cheated her, the daughter-in-law thought, and then I can prove to everyone in the village that she's just a fraud.

The old woman quickly realized what it was she had, but since she could not see Dove's portion, she assumed that the rest of the fish had been as bad as her daughter-in-law had claimed. Poor thing, the old woman thought to herself, she got cheated, so I won't embarrass her, poor dear. Besides, the old woman was the kind of person who found roses where others like Dove found only thorns.

"Hmm, yum," she declared. "The cheeks are the tastiest part. How is yours?"

Now Dove, who could see only thorns where others found roses, was sure that the old woman was trying to get her goat. "It's all right," she said in disappointment.

The next day, the old woman tried her best, but when she washed the clothes, they came out dirtier than before. Once again, a crowd gathered outside their house as Dove abused her mother-in-law, and once again, the young woman wound up quarreling with the neighbors.

As she had the day before, the old woman managed to make peace, and as she had the day before, Dove tested her by serving her the head of a fish that she had bought from the old fisherman. When the old woman praised it, Dove ground her teeth in exasperation.

Day after day that went on. For the sake of peace in the village, the old woman tried to help; but because her eyesight was bad, she kept making mistakes that sent Dove off into a tantrum. Each day, fearing for the old woman's life, the neighbors interfered, and Dove would then take them on.

Finally there came a day when even the old woman could not stand it anymore as Dove fought with their neighbors. Though the neighbors and the entire village were a blur to her, the old woman's feet remembered the way, and she stumbled out of the village. The fields were a hazy blend of browns and greens, but from the river's bank, she saw the sunlight shine upon the water so that it glittered like a golden road.

Sometimes falling from the dikes or tripping over

roots, she finally made her way to the riverbank, where she plopped down. There, alone and unseen by anyone, the old woman could worry in private. "What to do? What to do?" she fretted. "This used to be such a nice place. Now everyone's hoarse from arguing. And it's all my doing."

She stared at the water, and it seemed like a gleaming rug, woven of golden wires, that led straight up into heaven. She sighed heavily. "If I weren't here, everyone would have peace. I ought to just drown myself."

"You do," someone said, "and you'll spoil the fishing. How would it be if everyone jumped in the river when they felt like it? The poor fish would get so excited that they'd never eat—let alone nibble at a poor old man's hook."

The old woman squinted and made out the silhouette of an old man sitting on the bank beside her. She could just see the pale calves sticking out from under his dark, rolled-up trousers, and the straw hat covering his head. "Excuse me. I didn't see you." She started to get up. "I'll go away."

Holding on to his bamboo pole with one hand, he used his other to motion the old woman to sit back down. "Since you're here, you might as well stay. What's all that ruckus about up in the village?"

"They don't understand my daughter-in-law. She may say mean things, but she really treats me nicely.

She's always giving me the best portion of the fish."

"Is she now?" the old fisherman wondered, stroking his long, white beard.

"Yes. She knows I like the head because the cheeks are the tastiest portion of the fish."

The old fisherman sighed. "Well, you go home now. If she's as kind as you say, she must realize that our actions shape us. I'm sure she's sorry about the way she's treated you."

The old woman was desperate enough to grab at any hope. She got up immediately and started for the village.

On her way back, though, she thought over what the old man had said. "Perhaps," the old woman said, "our actions do shape us. Maybe he was trying to hint to me that it's my fault that she loses her temper. After all, my daughter-in-law must be tired of picking through all those bones for just a little bit of meat. Perhaps that's what puts her into such a bad temper."

When she returned home, she could smell the fish already cooked and waiting.

"Sit down," Dove said sullenly.

However, the old woman patted her arm. "It's not right that you give me the best part. Tonight, you get the fish head and I'll take what's left."

That was more than the daughter-in-law could bear. "If you aren't the most infuriating woman," the daughter-in-law shouted.

The insults brought out their neighbors, and once more the bewildered old woman fled to the river to weep, but as she sat there, she heard the kind voice of the fisherman. "Didn't things get better?" he asked.

The old woman shook her head. "I offered her the head, and now she's worse than ever." Suddenly she clutched at the old fisherman's sleeve. "Isn't there something you could do? You're so kind. Maybe if you talked to her, you could get her to calm down."

"Is that what you want?" the fisherman asked.

The old woman nodded toward the village. "I think we all do."

He took a small packet from his sleeve. "Then put this magical powder on your fish head."

"But how can that help her?" the old woman asked, puzzled.

"You'll see. Anyone who eats this powder reveals his true inner self to the world."

The old woman bowed and started for home, full of hope. Then, remembering her manners, she turned to thank the old man, but he was gone.

She blinked, squinting all around, but there wasn't a sign of him. "My eyesight must be getting worse," she decided.

When she reached home, she found that Dove had already reheated her supper. Remembering what the fisherman had said, the old woman opened the packet of powder, but she had no sooner begun to sprinkle it on the fish head when Dove snatched it from her hand. "What's this?"

"Something that will reveal our true selves."

"You're already a monstrous old hag," Dove snapped. Suspecting it might be poison, she put chopsticks into her mother-in-law's hand. "Go ahead and eat."

Before Dove threw another tantrum, the old woman snatched up her bowl and ate some of the fish head. "It really adds something to the flavor," the old woman said enthusiastically.

Dove watched the old woman carefully, and when she showed no ill effects, the daughter-in-law dumped the rest of the powder on her fish. "Well, even if it isn't magical, it ought to spice up our meal tonight."

The young woman took a bite. "Yes, it's really quite tasty." She took another bite. "Maybe you could get some more." She was just beginning to chew on a third mouthful when she dropped her chopsticks.

"Oh," she said. "Oh." She began to rub vigorously at her arms as if they itched uncontrollably.

"What is it?" Alarmed, the old woman got to her feet and groped along the table toward Dove. Though Dove seemed shorter than before, the old woman thought it was just a trick of her eyes. But when she reached out for her daughter-in-law, she touched warm golden fur.

With a gasp, the old woman started to pull back in fright, but she felt two small paws clutch at her arm and a monkey chattered at her fearfully. At once, the old woman realized what had happened. The powder had let the old woman stay as she was because she was already her true self, but it had brought out Dove's real nature. "You poor, poor thing," the old woman said, and took the monkey up in her arms.

Her neighbors helped the old woman after that. She would sit in a corner on her stool rocking the monkey in her arms, for the monkey had grown quite fond of the old woman and remained calm only while the old woman held her.

As one of neighbors whispered quietly to the others, Dove made a far better pet than human being.

The
Phantom
Heart

A long time ago there was a shopkeeper who hated children. When he and his wife couldn't have any children, he was rather relieved. But his wife talked about adopting someone. "I know you don't like children, but when we pass on, we need someone to send us food and money and all sorts of things."

The shopkeeper agreed, but said that they had plenty of time and kept postponing the moment. "When you're alive, there's no profit in children. They're dirty, noisy, wasteful creatures. And when you're dead, you're lucky if the ungrateful little things remember their duty."

His wife sighed in exasperation. "That's what I get for being married to the most practical man in the world."

"I am what I am," the shopkeeper insisted firmly,

71

"and I don't pretend to be any more."

Then one day when he left their house and went down to open up their shop, a little girl walked by, bearing a huge basket of fruit. As she trudged along, tears fell from her eyes.

"What's wrong?" the shopkeeper asked her.

She whirled like some startled bird, stared at him a moment, and then ran away as fast as she could with her burden of fruit.

The sad little girl made him feel as if there were truly something missing from his life. Finally, he slapped the side of his head and tried to laugh. "You're getting as flighty as a poet," he scolded himself. "Get ahold of yourself."

However, the rest of that day he went about his chores with only half a mind. He could not forget that sad little face. He spent the rest of the day puzzling over the girl. Why was she so sad? What was the poor thing afraid of?

And the shopkeeper, who prided himself upon being so sensible and down-to-earth, lay awake all night pondering the mystery that had stumbled into his life.

When he and his wife got up the next day, she studied him, worried. "You look like something the cat dragged in. Didn't you sleep well?"

"I had a lot on my mind," he mumbled.

She clicked her tongue. "I'll go to the herbalist and get some tea to help you sleep."

He was irritable from lack of sleep. "You think teas can solve everything!" he snapped at his startled wife.

He dressed quickly and ate a breakfast of cold rice and tea and hurried to his shop. Again he saw the little girl, and again she was crying. "What's wrong?" he asked her. "Is it indigestion?"

Fearfully, she looked all around as if she were afraid of being spied upon. Then, still weeping, she scurried away.

The third morning the sorrowful girl appeared at the same time as the other two days. Once more, she looked around with that sad, frightened face and almost stepped inside his shop. But fear made her stop and turn to go.

Just as she was leaving, the shopkeeper ran out of his shop. "Wait," he called. The little girl would have run like some frightened deer, but he caught her hand. "I've watched you for three mornings now. What's troubling you?"

She gazed at the shopkeeper and clasped his hand as if she were drowning. "You have such a kind face, I think you truly want to hear." Tears streamed from her eyes. "My parents were poor farmers. When they could no longer feed me, they sold me to a rich man. They did not want to, but it was either that or watch me starve. They couldn't know the rich man and his wife are cruel people. No matter how hard I try, I never satisfy them, and they beat me every day. I can't stand it anymore."

The shopkeeper was touched. "Perhaps we can find someone to buy your freedom."

"They are so disgusted with me, they say they would sell me for a handful of cash. But I don't even have that." The girl wept even harder, her hot tears falling upon his hand.

"Well, I do," the shopkeeper said. "Where do they live? I'll talk to them."

The girl bowed respectfully. "Lord, if you should go to them, they would ask far too much. However, if I were to break a few things today, they would be ready to kick me out. Then I might pretend the money is my life savings and buy my freedom."

The shopkeeper went inside and came out a moment later with a string of cash. "Take this, and good luck," he said.

Crying, the girl thanked him for his generosity and left. Idly, as he stared at the back of his hand, which was still moist with her tears, he realized what he had done. "Great Heavens. I've just given away money."

Stunned, he returned to his little shop and sat down on a stool. "She's probably some little thief who cheats fools like me. Well, I deserve it. Such nonsense is for shopkeepers as well as for poets. So the lesson is cheap at the price." And he had a good laugh at himself.

However, that very afternoon, the girl walked into his shop and presented herself. "Thank you. Now I'll work off my debt to you."

"But you're free," the shopkeeper protested.

The girl clutched the small basket of her belongings. "Did you ever think of what I was to do once I was free? Do you want me to become a beggar on the roads?"

"Of course not," the shopkeeper said, and scratched his head. "But what do I tell my wife?"

The girl looked around the little shop and then back at the shopkeeper. "She's the wife of a prosperous merchant—an important man in the town. It's time she started living like the wife of a man of substance. She shouldn't be doing the cooking and the washing and the cleaning. She should have a maid."

The shopkeeper was glad that the clever girl had given him an excuse, but his wife was annoyed when he repeated it to her. "We don't have any room," she told him.

"There's a long, narrow closet that I've been using as a storeroom. She can sleep there," the shopkeeper said hastily.

"I'll hire my own maid." His wife sniffed and went down to the store with every intention of firing the girl. However, when she saw how small and young she was, she softened. "She's hardly more than a baby," she whispered to her husband. "Let's see how good a maid she is."

The girl proved as respectful as anyone could ask and

did everything promptly and smartly. And she seemed to be exactly what she claimed to be: someone who was grateful to have a kind master and mistress.

The shopkeeper grew quite contented with himself for his good deed. Lately, he found himself sitting more and more. "I must be growing old," he said to himself. "It's good to have young legs around."

Then one day, when he was walking through town on an errand, he heard the fish clapper of a monk. A fish clapper was a kind of wooden knocker in the shape of a fish. Feeling especially virtuous, the shop-keeper stopped and took out some cash.

The monk stood there in an old yellow robe. Though his head was shaved, the elderly man had a wispy gray beard. As the shopkeeper made a show of putting the cash into the monk's begging bowl, the monk dropped his clapper and seized the man's wrist.

"Let me repay your kindness," the monk said. "People's faces are like pages in a book to me, and I can read their futures."

The shopkeeper, who liked to get his money's worth, told the monk to go ahead, but after a moment the monk sighed and shook his head. "You're going to die very soon."

Frightened, the shopkeeper felt his cheeks and jaws. "What's wrong with my face?"

"You're living with a monster," the monk stated calmly. "And the monster will kill you and make your ghost into its slave."

"But I live with my wife and our maid," the shop-keeper protested. "I've been with my wife for years without any trouble."

"Then it must be the maid," the monk said. "How have you been feeling lately?"

"I've been a little tired," the shopkeeper admitted, "but that's because I've been so busy in the shop."

The monk could feel the veins and arteries in the shopkeeper's wrist. "Your pulse is irregular. She's draining you. Beware of her." Releasing the shop-keeper, the monk picked up his clapper and started on.

The shopkeeper stood in a daze as he listened to the knocking of the clapper gradually fade into the dis-tance. He didn't know whether to believe the monk or not, but the monk had been so certain.

I'll ask her who her former master and mistress were, he said to himself. Then I can check up on her story and have a good laugh about that old monk.

Determined to prove his maid innocent, he returned home. As it happened, his wife was also out of the house. When the shopkeeper went to the maid's room, he found the door locked. From inside, there came an odd cackling sound. Puzzled, he sneaked around to the rear of the building.

The windows were of translucent rice paper in a frame of bamboo. Wetting his finger, he rubbed it against the rice paper so it became almost transparent.

Then he peeked inside.

Horrified, he saw a monster inside with long white hair flowing like withered old moss down its back to the floor. Wicked-looking fangs thrust out of its lower jaw, and its sunken eyes were as large as saucers and glowed a fiery red. When it raised a hand, he saw nails as long and sharp as daggers. Carefully the creature smoothed out a crisp roll of parchment. But as it unrolled on the floor, the shopkeeper realized it was not parchment at all but a human skin.

Dipping a long nail into a pot of ink, the creature smoothed out the skin and began to scratch out the outline of a human being. Once it had put in all the features, the monster sketched clothing over the human picture. Then it carefully picked up the painted skin, stretched it out, and put it on. Almost at once, the skin fitted itself snugly to the monster like a glove over a hand. And where the monster had once stood was now the young girl.

Horrified, the shopkeeper rounded up some of his neighbors and stormed into his own house, where the maid was calmly preparing lunch.

"You must go," he commanded.

The girl tried to take his hand. "Have I displeased you?"

"I order you out of this house," the shopkeeper insisted.

"I don't want to leave you," the girl insisted.

No matter how the girl protested, the shopkeeper refused to listen. Instead, he and his neighbors forced her out of the house. Packing up her few belongings, he dumped them outside and added a packet of money in the hopes of buying her off.

"Here, you can go anywhere now. Just leave my wife and me alone."

As he watched the little girl leave weeping so piteously, the shopkeeper almost changed his mind, but he reminded himself again of what he had seen. Once she was out of sight, he thanked his neighbors and locked up both his house and shop.

Naturally his strange behavior was the talk of the street, so his wife heard all about it before she actually unlocked their door and stepped inside.

The shopkeeper told her everything about the monster. "I was a fool," he confessed. "Can you ever forgive me for bringing that thing into the house?"

It was the first time she could remember her hard, practical husband ever apologizing. "With all my heart," she said, and stroked his cheek gently.

That night they locked up the house and shop tight, but nothing happened. However, the next night, a storm roared through the town. The wind shook the roofs like a wild animal while the rain clawed at the windows. Listening to the storm howl, he thought of the monk's prophecy that the monster would kill him. Frightened, the shopkeeper rolled over and put his arms around his wife. She asked him what was wrong; but the shopkeeper, who had once been hard-nosed, was now so afraid that he couldn't even utter a squeak. He could only hold on more tightly to his wife.

The storm returned the third night worse than ever. The rain crashed against the house like an ocean wave, and the roaring wind battered at the house like a giant bull. The house itself began to rock on its foundations like a ship in a stormy sea. Again, the shopkeeper clutched at his wife, and she tried to soothe him, though she herself felt afraid.

However, they had slept little the previous night, and so, even as frightened as they were, they eventually fell asleep despite the storm. As they lay now, side by side, the wind rose to a triumphant roar as it rocked the house back and forth.

Under cover of the storm, a little figure slid underneath the locked door. Darting across the floor, it jumped on top of the shopkeeper. With a quick slash of its claws, it laid open his chest and cut out his heart.

The next morning when the wife woke up and saw what had happened to her husband, she rushed out into the street, but before she could wake their neighbors, she saw the old monk.

The old monk scrutinized her face. "The fool is dead," he said. "Just as I predicted."

Remembering her husband's story, the woman fell on her knees. "Yes, he is, but I beg you to help him."

And she began to weep as she pleaded for her husband.

Touched by her love, the old monk sighed regretfully. "I'm afraid the monster's power is greater than mine." He pointed to a mountain. "But there is a master who lives upon that peak with enough magic to control even that monster." He paused and added, "It is a long journey, though."

"I would walk through fire," the wife insisted.

"And you must do whatever the master asks, no matter what," the monk warned.

"I will do whatever I need to do to save my husband," the wife promised.

Shutting up their house and shop, the woman set out at once. Following the monk's directions, she climbed the steep path, though her lungs and legs both ached. When she reached a waterfall, she turned right and entered into a little clearing. Just before the wet rocks was a dirty, ragged old beggar squatting on a boulder with his head tilted back, sunning himself like an old turtle.

"Is the master in?" she asked politely.

The old beggar did not even open his eyes. "I am the master, and I know why you came." When he scratched himself under his shirt, dirt pattered down in a little shower. "Will you do as I say?"

"Yes," the wife promised.

The old beggar kept scratching himself until he had a

ball of dirt in his hands. "Then eat this."

The wife stared at the disgusting lump in his clawlike hand. "I don't know if I can."

"Then you don't want my help," the beggar said, and threw it on the ground.

Gathering up her courage, the woman knelt and picked up the lump gingerly.

"Eat it, eat it, eat it!" the beggar began to chant.

Closing her eyes, she swallowed it in one gulp so as not to taste it.

From the boulder, the old beggar began to laugh crazily, but when she opened her eyes, he had slipped to the ground and was dashing up the rocky slope.

"Come back," she called after him. "You said you would help."

However, the old beggar, still cackling insanely, disappeared from view. The woman rose heavily. "He's no master—just some crazy old man playing a practical joke."

Discouraged, she made the long return journey to town. Plodding wearily into the bedroom, she knelt beside her husband. Instantly, her stomach began to cramp. "I tried to save you, but I couldn't," she apologized to her husband. "And now I'm sick."

She knelt there, weeping as she mourned for her husband, when suddenly the cramps grew more violent. Suddenly a warm object dropped out of her mouth. When she looked at it, she saw it was a heart.

"The old beggar did keep his promise," the wife said. Scooping up the heart, she set it carefully within her husband's chest. Instantly, the corpse began to twitch. Springing to her feet, the woman got her sewing basket. Taking out a needle and thread, she quickly sewed the heart into the chest.

For three days and nights, the shopkeeper lay there in the room, every now and then moving a limb or writhing on his back. On the fourth day, he woke and smiled up gratefully at his wife.

She fed him warm broth and bit by bit nursed him back to health. Even so, the slightest noise would wake him at night. "I keep thinking the monster will come back to fetch my new heart."

One day, the shopkeeper met the monk. After giving him a generous donation, the shopkeeper thanked him for all his advice and then confessed his anxieties.

"The monster will most certainly be back," the monk agreed. "Your wife had better journey to the mountain again and ask the master for his help a second time."

So the wife set out once more. When she met the old beggar by the falls, she begged for his help once more.

This time, he was as calm and reasonable as anybody on the street. From inside his ragged clothes, he pulled out a small black sack. Pasted on the sack was a red sign with magical words written on it. "Open this when you see the monster; and when you've caught it, burn the creature, sack, paper, and charm."

Thanking the beggar, the wife returned to her husband. For three nights, they sat up anxiously, waiting for the monster to come. Then on the fourth, the storm came. The wind rattled the roof tiles, and sheets of water drummed against the windows.

And at the height of the storm, the little figure slipped under the door once again. As it started to race across the floor, the woman held up the little black sack toward the monster. Instantly, a hand shot out of the sack, stretching across the floor on a rubbery arm that never seemed to end.

With a tiny shriek, the monster tried to turn and run, but too late. The hand snatched up the creature and pulled it back inside the sack. Immediately, the shopkeeper and his wife took it down to the kitchen, where they had the stove all prepared. Lighting the fire, they threw the sack into it.

Monster, sack, and hand disappeared in a burst of fire. As the ashes went whirling outside, the storm stopped instantly.

High on his mountaintop, the beggar had stood waiting. Now he cupped his dirty palms together and gathered the ashes, burying them in a special spot he had picked out on the mountain.

Whether it was his new heart or gratitude to his wife, the shopkeeper didn't argue when she said she wanted to adopt a baby. To his shock, he found he rather liked being a father and suggested they adopt another one.

His surprised wife stared at him. "What's gotten into you?"

"I can't give you a practical reason why," he said, and tapped his chest. "It must be this new heart. I don't think it works right."

But, in fact, it was working quite well.

The Wild Heart

Living in a strange land is a bit like walking along on a tight-rope. A mistake in balance leads to a fall, and so moderation is a tactic of survival—especially where things could turn hostile, as they often did in America. Besides many discriminatory laws, there were actual riots from the 1890's by the mobs trying to drive the Chinese away.

A sense of cooperation was vital in a country where the Chinese frequently could depend only upon their own people, as in "The Snake's Revenge."

Charity was also a virtue even more necessary for Chinese Americans. We are all strangers in a strange land, and sometimes kindness does pay off, as in "Waters of Gold."

For centuries, a farmer's world was defined by the area be-

86

tween village fields and market town. In that limited world, there were many ways for a society to curb wild behavior. Shame was frequently a mechanism. When it didn't work, as in "The Foolish Wish," the consequences could be lethal.

However, when these young Chinese came to America, many of the usual social restraints were no longer present, despite the organization of family and district associations. "Tiger Cat" warns that the most harmless creature may contain a beast—a beast that can be contained only with constant watchfulness.

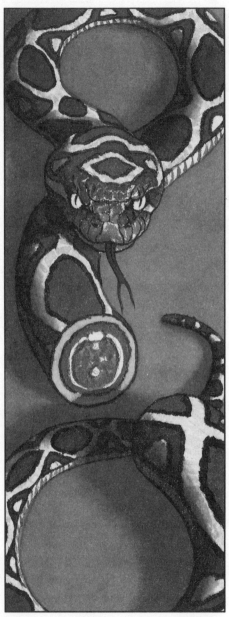

The
Snake's
Revenge

Many years ago there was a hunter named Leaf who lived deep in the woods. In front of his small house grew wild fig trees that drew birds of so many colors that sometimes the branches seemed filled with rainbows. Dark moss swayed as it hung from spice trees that scented the little clearing around his house. Here, among chattering birds and long-armed, whistling monkeys, he would wake every morning and think himself the luckiest person alive.

Humming to himself, Leaf would duck his head under the low doorway and step outside to wash his face in the stream that splashed merrily near his house.

Then, gathering his nets and his crossbow, he would set out through the soft green light of the forest. Steam rose from the damp floor of the forest, rising in ribbons that wriggled upward toward the green jungle canopy high overhead.

Leaf killed; but he never killed needlessly, because he loved the woods so much. The few people who knew him said that he must have been a forest animal in some other life.

However, one day he had no luck hunting. Feeling tired and disappointed, he started for home on a winding animal track. Hidden by a bend was a large poisonous snake taking a nap right across the trail.

When the hunter stepped onto a twig, the loud snap woke the snake. With a loud angry hiss, it reared up and opened its mouth to strike, but as soon as the hunter had seen the gleam of poisoned fangs, he had drawn his large knife. Quickly swinging, he chopped the snake in half. Both parts flopped back on the ground, wriggling frantically.

Drawing back a step, Leaf waited until each half of the snake was still. Thinking that the snake was dead and counting himself lucky to have survived, Leaf stepped around both pieces and started on once again.

However, the upper portion of the snake was still alive, and one thought kept going through its mind over and over: He will die in more pain than I.

Since it knew where the hunter lived, it began to crawl through the bushes, painfully, slowly. As it struggled toward the house, its blood kept pumping out and mixing with the dirt and dry sand, and the wound became covered with red mud. Eventually, its severed end became coated with so many layers that there was a ball-like lump the size of a fist at that end.

In the meantime, Leaf had hiked on, unaware that the snake was still very much alive. He followed the path as it twisted through the thickest, darkest portion of the woods. As he walked, he was careful to watch for more poisonous snakes. Even so, he was surprised when he saw a woman sitting beside the trail.

She was small and dark and old, and twigs and old leaves were snagged in her long, bushy gray hair. Though it was a dry day, she wore a raincoat of woven straw that had grown muddy with age, and her trousers were more moss than cloth.

When she saw him, she held up a grimy palm. "I hear a jingle that gives me a tingle."

The woman looked so old and ragged that Leaf felt sorry for her. "What happened to your family, Auntie?"

"It's a story too long, full of woe and wrong."

Leaf was already digging into his pouch. "You'd find better pickings in town than in the middle of the woods."

"All the same, you came." She thrust a dirty palm at him.

Leaf handed her what money he had. "Here, Auntie. You need these coins more than I do."

As she clasped the money to her, the old woman struggled to her feet with a smile. "If you could have a wish, no matter how outlandish, what would it be? You can tell me."

Leaf scratched his head. "There may be folk richer than me and there are certainly folk better-looking than me," he admitted, "but there is no one luckier than me. If you were to give me a fortune, I'd still be doing exactly what I was doing. All I want to do is go on living in the woods." And that realization made him feel good inside.

"Lucky the person who has so much fun he would not change places with anyone. In the green wood, your life is charmed. Stay here and you'll never be harmed."

Muttering other such reassuring words, the old woman slipped into the shadowy trees like a carp disappearing into the green depths of a pool.

"These woods are beginning to get a little crowded if we've got poets and beggars," Leaf muttered to himself. "Maybe it's time to be moving deeper into the woods."

By this time, the snake had reached the hunter's house. More dead than alive, it started to wriggle toward a fig tree to hide; and then it saw a small hole in a wall of the house, close to the door. I'll surprise him even better if I can hide inside, the snake thought, and with one last burst of energy, it crawled toward the hole. Though it managed to get its head and part of its body through, the lump of red mud stuck in the hole, and the snake was so weak by now that it could not pull free.

The snake looked around the dark house. Despite the ball of mud, it was far enough inside. "When the man returns, I will bite him and kill him."

Nursing its strength, the snake lay as still as a dead branch, dreaming of the joyful moment when it would sink its fangs into the leg of the man.

As the twilight deepened in the woods, Leaf finally caught sight of his house. "It will be good to get off these old, aching feet of mine." And he hurried along eagerly.

Picking some figs from the trees, he was just about to stumble inside when he saw a flash of bright blue. Turning, he saw a kingfisher land on the ground and begin to bite the wildflowers that grew near a wall of his house. It was such an odd sight that the hunter stopped to watch.

At first, he thought the kingfisher might be chasing some bugs there, but its sharp beak grasped each flower by the stalk and with a quick bite cut through the stem. When it had harvested a dozen flowers, it gathered them up with difficulty. Rising into the air, it left the bouquet by the base of the wall and flew away.

"Now I've seen everything," Leaf grunted. Walking over to the wall, he was just about to pick up the bouquet when he noticed the red lump of dirt.

Curious, he tiptoed even closer, but he still could not

make out what the lump of mud was doing there.

Suspicious now, he quietly shed his hunting gear and slid out his great knife. Reaching down cautiously, he grasped the red ball of mud and yanked. Out slid the snake into the open.

Though the snake was surprised, it twisted upward with its last energy for one final lunge. However, Leaf was quicker. With a slash of his knife, he lopped off the head of the snake. Instantly, the body went limp, though the snake's jaws kept opening and closing among the flowers.

When the fangs were finally still, Leaf made a fire on a patch of dirt and with a stick shoved the now motionless head into the flames and then flung the body in after it.

As his enemy burned, Leaf felt a breeze brush his ear as gently as a kiss. "In the green wood, your life is charmed. Stay here and you'll never be harmed," a voice said from the air.

Leaf looked all around, but saw only the darkening woods around him. Then he knew that the old woman had been some spirit of the woods. For his act of kindness, she had protected him.

The Foolish Wish

Many years ago there was a boy named Turtle who could think only about girls. His father complained, "It's all I can do to get you to work in the fields to grow the rice you eat. But the moment my back is turned, you're weeding someone else's field while you flirt with some girl."

Ashamed, Turtle promised to behave, but on the way to the fields, he saw a girl kneeling by the well, washing clothes. In the fields, he could think only of her, until he couldn't bear it any longer. Finally, he asked his brother to make excuses for him, and he sneaked back to the village.

Though the family farmed about an acre of land, it was divided into five strips scattered around the valley floor; therefore, it was hard for his father to check on him if his brother said Turtle was at some distant field.

97

At the end of the day, though, all the mothers in the village were waiting at the gate as his father trudged up the road. "None of our girls got any washing done, and it's all your son's fault."

Embarrassed, the father promised that it would not happen again. His son was at home with water freshly drawn from the well so his father and brother could clean themselves.

"You're not stupid, so I know you understand me." His father sighed. "And you're not a liar, so I think you mean it when you promise to change."

"I do, Father," Turtle said. "I really mean to work and not bother anyone; but then my curiosity gets to itching. I hear a lovely laugh and I want to see the face that goes with the laugh."

"Then the only thing to do," his father said, as he began to splash water over his sweaty, hot face, "is to keep you with me all the time."

The next day, his father made sure his son was always within sight, and as a result, they and everyone else in the village got a surprising amount of work done.

However, Turtle was so exhausted by a full day of work that he had to rest by the road leading to the village. Everyone else, including his father, had gone on ahead, but his brother sat down to keep him company and admire the sunset.

Turtle slumped in the dirt. "I'm hot, I'm tired,

and"—he groaned—"we still have that long walk back home."

His brother fanned the air with his hand to try to cool him off a bit. "You'll feel better in a moment."

Suddenly Turtle sat bolt upright and stared. A young girl was walking on the road. In her dainty hands, she held a huge red parasol painted with flowers that hid her head and shoulders. Her jacket was of yellow silk patterned with red birds, and her light-blue skirt was pleated at the waist, each pleat with a ruffle of a different color. When a breeze puffed it out, the skirt belled outward like a halo around the moon.

"I didn't think anyone like her lived near our village." Turtle gaped.

His brother couldn't help staring too. "Why is she hiding her face?"

Turtle waved a hand in a worldly way. "Fool, a girl of quality doesn't want to be tanned like some common field hand. I wonder what she looks like."

When he started to get up, his brother pulled him back down. "You're the fool. If she really is quality, why would she speak to the likes of us?"

So they stayed where they were, watching as she walked up the road past the village and out of sight.

All that night and the next day, Turtle could not get the girl out of his mind. "I wouldn't have to talk with her," he said. "I would only have to see her face."

Once again, Turtle and his brother were the last ones

to head homeward, and Turtle sat down on the ground. "She might not come by," his brother warned.

Turtle thrust his feet out in front of himself, and tried to wipe the sweat and dirt from his face with his sleeve to make himself more presentable. "I'll take that chance."

Though his brother was tired and wanted to go home, he sat down to wait too. "Someone has to keep you from making a fool out of yourself."

The girl appeared again. Slender and graceful, she seemed to float along the road, her skirt rippling as she walked.

"Lady," Turtle called to her before his brother clapped a hand over his mouth.

The girl strolled by with the parasol between herself and the two boys as if they were not there. Or if she saw them, she was too well bred to answer.

Turtle was quite red-faced from trying to free himself from his brother's grip. By the time his brother let go, the girl was gone. "I'd give my life to know what she looks like," he complained.

His brother was just as flushed from the struggle. He wrung the hand that his brother had bitten. "Be careful what you wish."

"Someone that graceful must also have a lovely face," Turtle insisted.

His brother took him by the hand and pulled him to his feet. "Come on. Supper's waiting." And he tugged

Turtle along the road toward the village. And since Turtle kept stealing desperate looks over his shoulder, his brother kept hold of his hand to keep him from straying into the nearest ditch.

That evening, as Turtle lay on the straw mat listening to his brother and father snore, he made up his mind. If I have to go one more night without seeing her face, he said to himself, I'll explode.

So the next day, late in the afternoon, he made a point of going home early to get supper ready for his family. Rushing to the village, he got everything ready and then asked a neighbor woman to tell his father and brother when they returned that Turtle had gone to another part of the village to borrow some cooking oil for tomorrow.

Then Turtle darted out of the village and hid in some bushes until his father and brother had both passed by. Washing his face in a stream, and trying to dust his clothes, he went back to wait at his usual spot.

The girl appeared at the same time as before, twirling her parasol in her hand so that the flowers seemed to dance in a slow circle. Turtle called to her; but she strolled right on as if he did not exist. As he watched the girl almost float away from him, desperation made him grow bolder. Jumping to his feet, he trotted after her.

When she heard his footsteps, the girl started to hurry, and Turtle had to quicken his own pace, until both of them were racing along the road. "She has very strong legs," he thought, panting.

Though his own shoulders were heaving, she didn't show any strain at all. With one final determined burst of speed, Turtle caught up with her. "Now I'm going to see your face at last." And he hopped to her left.

Just as nimbly, the girl swung her parasol in front of him. Turtle jumped to her right; but once more the girl was too quick for him.

At the same time, the girl resolutely continued on so that Turtle pranced back and forth across the road like a frog zigging and zagging. However, try as hard as he could, he saw only black hair, pale hands, and the red circle of the parasol.

Exasperated, Turtle finally grabbed the parasol itself and yanked it out of her hands. He expected to see a face whose beauty would outshine everyone's. Instead, he saw a grotesque face leering evilly as a long red tongue wriggled in the air like a snake.

Turtle stood there frozen as the slender body suddenly began to melt into a slimy lump, the shining black hair stretching into straggling wirelike wisps and the pale hands arching into sharp-tipped claws.

When the monster reached for the boy, he thrust the parasol into its gaping mouth. As paper and sticks crunched, Turtle whirled around and began to run. He had been so busy trying to sneak a peek at the face that he had not noticed it had lured him into a cemetery.

He tripped over an old, open coffin and sprawled on his face.

At that moment, his father and brother came up the road, having finally figured out that Turtle had been trying to see the strange girl's face. Though afraid, they shouted and charged toward the monster. Distracted, the monster turned long enough to let Turtle get to his feet and race out of the cemetery, and then all three bolted back to the village. Behind them, they heard a loud screech, as if a soul were being torn in half.

As the first candles were being lit in the houses, they stumbled through the village gate calling to the others. While they stood there panting, the villagers tumbled into the lane to see what was wrong.

When they had explained, a wise old man said, "It must be some kind of ghost that comes out of its coffin. We must destroy it before it destroys us. But it could be dangerous, so let this be a task for the old men who can no longer work in the fields. This is one more thing we can do for the village."

A dozen old men said they would go; but no one slept well that night. And Turtle did not sleep at all. He felt as if he had a great stone pressing down on his chest and heart.

The next morning, the elderly volunteers stepped outside armed with sticks. One of them had even brought along a jar of oil. As they moved toward the village gate, they found Turtle waiting. "I know where the spot is," he said.

So Turtle led them to the cemetery. Quietly they crept among the graves until they reached the spot where the open coffin had been. The casket lay only a few inches beneath the surface, so it was easy to expose it. Lifting the jar, they upended it so that oil gushed out over the coffin. Then, with tinder and flint, they set the wooden planks on fire. The old, dry wood caught instantly. As the flames rose upward, Turtle began to feel as if the weight had suddenly dissolved and his heart was free, and he felt as if he were just waking from a dream.

Sad to say, the encounter did not end Turtle's flirting, but after that he was certainly much more careful about what he wished.

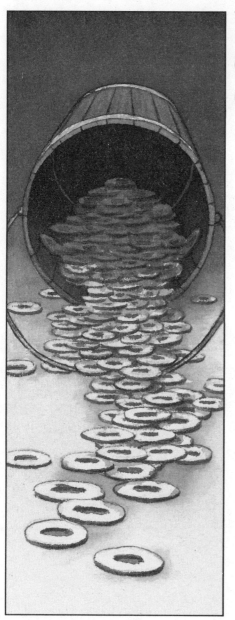

Waters
of
Gold

Many years ago, there lived a woman whom everyone called Auntie Lily. She was Auntie by blood to half the county and Auntie to the other half by friendship. As she liked to say, "There's a bit of Heaven in each of us." As a result, she was always helping people out.

Because of her many kind acts, she knew so many people that she couldn't go ten steps without meeting someone who wanted to chat. So it would take her half the day to go to the village well and back to her home.

Eventually, though, she helped so many people that she had no more money. She had to sell her fields and even her house to her neighbor, a rich old woman. "If you'd helped yourself instead of others, you wouldn't have to do this," the neighbor said smugly. "Where are all those other people when you need them?"

"That isn't why I helped them," Auntie Lily said firmly. She wound up having to pay rent for the house she had once owned. She supported herself by her embroidery; but since her eyes were going bad, she could not do very much.

One day an old beggar entered the village. He was a ragbag of a man—a trash heap, a walking pig wallow. It was impossible to tell what color or what shape his clothes had once been, and his hair was as muddy and matted as a bird's nest. As he shuffled through the village gates, he called out, "Water for my feet. Please, water for my feet. One little bowl of water—that's all I ask."

Everyone ignored him, pretending to concentrate on their chores instead. One man went on replacing the shaft of his hoe. A woman swept her courtyard. Another woman fed her hens.

The beggar went to each in turn, but they all showed their backs to him.

After calling out a little while longer, the beggar went to the nearest home, which happened to belong to the rich old woman. When he banged at her door, he left the dirty outline of his knuckles on the clean wood. And when the rich woman opened her door, his smell nearly took her breath away.

Now it so happened that she had been chopping vegetables when the beggar had knocked. When the beggar repeated his request, she raised her cleaver menacingly. "What good would one bowl of water be? You'd need a whole river to wash you clean. Go away."

"A thousand pardons," the old beggar said, and shambled on to the next house.

Though Auntie Lily had to hold her nose, she asked politely, "Yes?"

"I'd like a bowl of water to wash my feet." And the beggar pointed one grimy finger toward them.

Her rich neighbor had stayed in her doorway to watch the beggar. She scolded Auntie Lily now. "It's all your fault those beggars come into the village. They know they can count on a free meal."

It was an old debate between them, so Auntie Lily simply said, "Any of us can have bad luck."

"Garbage," the rich old woman declared, "is garbage. They must have done something bad, or Heaven wouldn't have let them become beggars."

Auntie Lily turned to the beggar. "I may be joining you on the road someday. Wait here."

Much to the neighbor's distress, Auntie Lily went inside and poured water from a large jar in her kitchen into a bucket. Carrying it in both hands, she brought it outside to the beggar and set it down.

The beggar stood on one leg, just like a crane, while he washed one callused, leathery sole over the bucket. "You can put mud on any other part of me, but if my feet are clean, then I feel clean."

As he fussily continued to cleanse his feet, Auntie Lily asked kindly, "Are you hungry? I don't have much, but what I have I'm willing to share."

The beggar shook his head. "I've stayed longer in this village than I have in any other. Heaven is my roof, and the whole world my house."

Auntie Lily stared at him, wondering what she would look like after a few years on the road. "Are you very tired? Have you been on the road for very long?"

"No, the road is on me," the beggar said, and held up his hands from his dirty sides. "But thank you. You're the first person to ask. And you're the first person to give me some water. So place the bucket of water by your bed tonight and do not look into it till tomorrow morning."

As the beggar shuffled out of the village again, Auntie Lily stared down doubtfully at the bucket of what was now muddy water. Then, even though she felt foolish, she picked it up again.

"You're not really going to take that scummy water inside?" laughed the rich neighbor. "It'll probably breed mosquitoes."

"It seemed important to him," she answered. "I'll humor him."

"Humoring people," snapped the neighbor, "has got you one step from begging yourself."

However, Auntie Lily carried the bucket inside anyway. Setting it down near her sleeping mat, she covered the mouth of the bucket with an old, cracked plate so she wouldn't peek into it by mistake, and then she got so caught up in embroidering a pair of slippers that she forgot all about the beggar and his bucket of water.

She sewed until twilight, when it was too dark to use her needle. Then, because she had no money for oil or candles, she went to sleep.

The next morning Auntie Lily rose and stretched the aches out of her back. She sighed. "The older I get, the harder it is to get up in the morning."

She was always saying something like that, but she had never stayed on her sleeping mat—even when she was sick. Thinking of all that day's chores, she decided to water the herbs she had growing on one side of her house.

Her eyes fell upon the beggar's bucket with its covering plate. "No sense using fresh water when that will do as well. After all, dirt's dirt to a plant."

Squatting down, she picked up the bucket and was surprised at how heavy it was. "I must have filled it fuller than I thought," she grunted.

She staggered out of the house and over to the side where rows of little green herbs grew. "Here you go," she said to her plants. "Drink deep."

Taking off the plate, she upended the bucket; but instead of muddy brown water, there was a flash of reflected light and a clinking sound as gold coins rained down upon her plants.

Auntie Lily set the bucket down hastily and crouched, not trusting her weak eyes. However, where some of her herbs had been, there was now a small mound of gold coins. She squinted in disbelief and rubbed her aching eyes and stared again; but the gold was still there.

She turned to the bucket. There was even more gold inside. Scooping up coins by the handful, she freed her little plants and made sure that the stalks weren't too bent.

Then she sat gazing at her bucket full of gold until a farmer walked by. "Tell me I'm not dreaming," she called to him.

The farmer yawned and came over with his hoe over his shoulder. "I wish I were dreaming, because that would mean I'm still in bed instead of having to go off to work."

Auntie Lily gathered up a handful of gold coins and let it fall in a tinkling, golden shower back into the bucket. "And this is real?"

The farmer's jaw dropped. He picked up one coin with his free hand and bit into it. He flipped it back in with the other coins. "It's as real as me, Auntie. But where did you ever get that?"

So Auntie Lily told him. And as others woke up and stepped outside, Auntie told them as well, for she still could not believe her luck and wanted them to confirm that the gold was truly gold. In no time at all, there was a small crowd around her.

If the bucket had been filled with ordinary copper cash, that would have been more money than any of them had ever seen. In their wildest dreams, they had never expected to see that much gold. Auntie Lily stared at the bucket uncomfortably. "I keep thinking it's going to disappear the next moment."

The farmer, who had been standing there all this time, shook his head. "If it hasn't disappeared by now, I don't think it will. What are you going to do with it, Auntie?"

Auntie Lily stared at the bucket, and suddenly she came to a decision. Stretching out a hand, she picked up a gold coin. "I'm going to buy back my house, and I'm going to get back my land."

The farmer knew the fields. "Those old things? You could buy a valley full of prime land with half that bucket. And a palace with the other half."

"I want what I sweated for." Asking the farmer to guard her bucket, Auntie Lily closed her hand around the gold coin. Then, as the crowd parted before her, she made her way over to her neighbor.

Now the rich old woman liked to sleep late; but all the noise had woken her up, so she was just getting dressed when Auntie knocked. The old woman yanked her door open as she buttoned the last button of her coat. "Who started the riot? Can't a person get a good night's sleep?"

With some satisfaction, Auntie Lily held up the gold coin. "Will this buy back my house and land?"

"Where did you get that?" the old woman demanded.

"Will it buy them back?" Auntie Lily repeated.

The rich old woman snatched the coin out of Auntie Lily's hand and bit into it just as the farmer had. "It's real," the old woman said in astonishment.

"Will it?" Auntie asked again.

"Yes, yes, yes," the old woman said crabbily. "But where did you ever get that much gold?"

When Auntie Lily told her the story and showed her the bucket of gold, the rich old woman stood moving her mouth like a fish out of water. Clasping her hands together, she shut her eyes and moaned in genuine pain. "And I sent him away. What a fool I am. What a fool." And the old woman beat her head with her fists.

That very afternoon, the beggar—the ragbag, the trash heap, the walking pig wallow—shuffled once more through the village gates with feet as dirty as before. As he went, he croaked, "Water for my feet. Please, water for my feet. One little bowl of water—that's all I ask."

This time, people dropped whatever they were doing when they heard his plea. Hoes, brooms, and pots were flung down, hens and pigs were kicked out of the way as everyone hurried to fill a bucket with water. There was a small riot by the village well as everyone fought to get water at the same time. Still others rushed out with buckets filled from the jars in their houses.

"Here, use my water," one man shouted, holding up a tub.

A woman shoved in front of him with a bucket in her arms. "No, no, use mine. It's purer."

They surrounded the old beggar, pleading with him to use their water, and in the process of jostling one another, they splashed a good deal of water on one another and came perilously close to drowning the beggar. The rich old woman, Auntie Lily's neighbor, charged to the rescue.

"Out of the way, you vultures," the rich old woman roared. "You're going to trample him." Using her elbows, her feet, and in one case even her teeth, the old woman fought her way through the mob.

No longer caring if she soiled her hands, the old woman seized the beggar by the arm. "This way, you poor, misunderstood creature."

Fighting off her neighbors with one hand and keeping her grip on the beggar with the other, the old woman hauled him inside her house. Barring the door against the rest of the village, she ignored all the fists and feet thumping on her door and all the shouts.

"I really wasn't myself yesterday, because I had been up the night before tending a sick friend. This is what I meant to do." She fetched a fresh new towel and an even newer bucket and forced the beggar to wash his feet.

When he was done, he handed her the now filthy towel. "Dirt's dirt, and garbage is garbage," he said.

However, the greedy old woman didn't recognize her own words. She was too busy trying to remember what else Auntie Lily had done. "Won't you have something to eat? Have you traveled very far? Are you tired?" she asked, all in the same breath.

The old beggar went to the door and waited patiently while she unbarred it. As he shuffled outside, he instructed her to leave the bucket of water by her bed but not to look into it until the morning.

That night, the greedy old woman couldn't sleep as she imagined the heap of shiny gold that would be waiting for her tomorrow. She waited impatiently for the sun to rise and got up as soon as she heard the first rooster crow.

Hurrying to the bucket, she plunged her hands inside expecting to bring up handfuls of gold. Instead, she gave a cry as dozens of little things bit her, for the bucket was filled not with gold but with snakes, lizards, and ants.

The greedy old woman fell sick—some said from her bites, some claimed from sheer frustration. Auntie Lily herself came to nurse her neighbor. "Take this to heart: Kindness comes with no price."

The old woman was so ashamed that she did, indeed, take the lesson to heart. Though she remained sick, she was kind to whoever came to her door.

One day, a leper came into the village. Everyone hid for fear of the terrible disease. Doors slammed and shutters banged down over windows, and soon the village seemed deserted.

Only Auntie Lily and her neighbor stepped out of their houses. "Are you hungry?" Auntie Lily asked.

"Are you thirsty?" the neighbor asked. "I'll make you a cup of tea."

The leper thanked Auntie Lily and then turned to the neighbor as if to express his gratitude as well; but he stopped and studied her. "You're looking poorly, my dear woman. Can I help?"

With a tired smile, the rich old woman explained what had happened. When she was finished, the leper stood thoughtfully for a moment. "You're not the same woman as before: You're as kind as Auntie Lily, and you aren't greedy anymore. So take this humble gift from my brother, the old beggar."

With that, the leper limped out of the village; and as he left, the illness fell away from the old woman like an old, discarded cloak. But though the old woman was healthy again, she stayed as kind as Auntie Lily and used her own money as well and wisely as Auntie Lily used the waters of gold.

The
Tiger
Cat

Many years ago, when the jungle covered much of southern China, there was a boy named Bugsy. His father had been a Chinese soldier, but his mother was from one of the tribes of the area. As a result, when his parents died, nobody wanted him.

Climbing high into the mountains, he would cut firewood and carry it down to sell in the villages. It was a hard life because he never got much for the wood he cut; and it was a lonely life because he never saw anyone. And when he went into the villages, the children would make fun of his ragged clothes.

One day, as he searched for wood, Bugsy wound up in a part of the jungle he had never been in before. There, the wood was plentiful, and he began to make up his loads, gathering the wood into two big stacks to hang from either end of a bamboo pole.

Squatting, Bugsy got his shoulder under the pole and staggered to his feet. He had not gone more than a mile through the trees when he came upon an old man sitting upon a basket and fanning himself with a big, broad leaf he had broken off from a nearby plant.

The old man's robes were nearly as ragged and dirty as Bugsy's. "B-b-boy," he stuttered. "Y-y-you have such young legs, and I have such old legs. Will you help me?"

Now Bugsy wanted to return to town with his load of firewood because he had wandered so far that day, but he felt sorry for the old man. "Is it very far?" the boy asked.

"N-n-no, not very far," the old man said.

So Bugsy agreed. Leaving his wood near a tree, he went over to the old man. As he got up close, he noticed that the old man's skin was as smooth and wrinkle free as a baby's. When the old man got up, Bugsy saw that the basket was filled with red rocks. "How did you carry this, old man?"

"I d-d-don't know myself," the old man said, rubbing his back.

Bugsy had to get his pole and take off one bundle of firewood so he could balance the load of rocks on that end.

The old man was already walking away and waving at him impatiently. "It's th-th-this way."

Bugsy stumbled after the old man, but after a mile

he panted, "Is it much farther?"

The old man had kept hold of his leafy fan, which he still waved at himself. "D-d-don't tell me you're getting tired already."

At the end of every new mile, Bugsy asked the old man if they would reach his hut soon, and each time the old man replied it was only a little farther, until eventually they reached a mountain with two peaks.

By then, the jungle had begun to grow darker. And the monkeys began to howl, and the elephants to trumpet, and the birds to screech. And Bugsy knew that when the jungle was this noisy, it meant it was twilight, the time the animals wake and begin to search for food.

As the jungle darkened around him, Bugsy could barely see in front of him; yet the old man kept moving on as before. "Wait, we should climb a tree," the boy called. He ducked his head under what he thought was a vine hanging down from a branch, but the vine began to slither and drop a coil around him.

However, the old man had come back for him. Seizing the snake, he yanked it out of the tree and tossed it absentmindedly into a bush. "This way. It's just a little farther." Holding on to the carrying pole, the old man guided Bugsy up the wooded slopes until they lurched into a small clearing before a small, rickety hut made of bamboo poles lashed together with vines and wild brambles.

"W-w-welcome to my humble home," the old man said. "I c-c-can manage from here."

As the jungle shrieked and roared around him, Bugsy shuddered. "I'll never get home now."

"Af-f-fraid of the dark, are you?" the old man chuckled. "Well, you can stay at my house for the night." Carefully he opened the door.

Bugsy wasn't sure if the strange old man's hut was any safer than the jungle, but since he did not seem to have much choice, he set his pole down, got the basket, and followed the old man inside.

There was already a fire banked in a little brick stove in one corner that cast a blood-red light around the walls. The hut was filled with beakers and jars and books with strange symbols. The air inside the hut reeked of chemicals, but the old man didn't seem to notice. "Put the basket over by the stove," he instructed, and closed the door quickly behind the boy.

By now, though, Bugsy was ready to risk a jungle full of snakes rather than stay cooped up in the old man's hut. When he saw two pairs of green eyes leave one corner, he gave a yell. The next moment, he saw they were two small furry creatures striped like the shadows of the jungle.

As he stood there petrified, the little creatures rubbed themselves against his legs and began to make a strange vibrating sound from deep within their bodies.

"What is that weird noise?" the terrified Bugsy

asked. "It sounds like they're going to explode."

"I c-c-call that purring," the old man said. "That means my little jewels like you."

Setting the basket down, Bugsy clumsily patted one of the animals. "What are they?"

"They're k-k-kittens." The old man squatted down and stroked them gently. "And you don't pat them like big, ugly dogs. They're much more s-s-subtle creatures."

Fetching some of the rocks from the basket, the old man began to putter at his stove, leaving Bugsy to himself. Against one wall was a dirty straw mat, where Bugsy lay down. Almost immediately, the two kittens snuggled up against him, one on his belly and the other in his arms. When both began to purr again, Bugsy found he liked it.

The old man fed the fire in the stove until strange shadows danced around the walls of the hut, and Bugsy watched as the old man crushed the rock and melted it down until it made a shining silver liquid.

Uneasily Bugsy thought that perhaps he should leave the hut, but he was worn out from his journey, and the two kittens were warm and soft and their purring seemed to pass from their bodies into his. So, among the odd fumes and shadows, the boy fell asleep.

When he woke the next morning, the old man was still at the stove. When Bugsy tried to sit up, the two kittens meowed in complaint. Instantly, the old man turned around. "M-m-my jewels seem to have taken to you. When I get deep into my studies, I forget all about them. Perhaps they'd be better off with you."

Bugsy looked down at the two bundles of fur, which had readjusted themselves to his lap. If I had the kittens, he thought, I'd never be lonely again.

"How can you bear to part with them?" Bugsy asked.

The old man paused with a beaker in his hand. "It w-w-won't be easy," the old man said, "but I want them to be happy. There's only one thing. Keep them in your house and never, ever let them get loose in the jungle."

"I'd hate for some snake to make them into a dinner," Bugsy agreed. He asked the old man for a basket, and the old man waved his beaker around the house.

"I think th-th-there's an empty one in here someplace," the old man said.

As Bugsy rummaged around, the old man gave him some quick instructions on how to care for the boy's new pets. Once Bugsy had found an empty basket and cleaned it out, he stowed his precious cargo in it. They complained quite loudly when he set the lid over them, making the boy feel guilty. "Maybe I'd better leave the lid open a crack."

The old man whirled around. "N-n-no! I told you: Don't let them loose in the jungle."

Afraid that the old man would take back his gift, Bugsy promised fervently to protect his pets. Then,

leaving the old man inside the hut, the boy went outside and hung the basket from the empty end of the
pole. Because the kittens were so much lighter than
the wood, he had to adjust the position of the basket,
but eventually he had it balanced so he could set out
again.

Just as Bugsy was about to leave, the old man called
from within the hut, "Remember: K-k-keep them
locked up. There's a bit of wildness in every beast."

Bugsy returned to the spot where he had left the
other bundle of wood and added that to the pole.
Though the load was now awkward with the wood
and the basket, he managed to make it into town.
Once he had sold all his wood, he bought liver and
other special little treats for his new companions—
though Bugsy himself would have to go hungry that
night.

Immediately, he set out for home so he could shut
them up safely in his hut. However, the kittens were
still protesting loudly at being cooped up in the basket,
and Bugsy, who had never owned anything before,
wanted to hold them and make them purr once more.

So, sitting down, he lifted up the lid. Inside, the two
kittens rose on their hindlegs, setting their paws on the
edge. One kitten was all eyes for its master, but the
other kitten only stared at the surrounding jungle.

When a parrot screeched overhead, the first kitten
leaped out of the basket and huddled against its mas-

ter, but the second kitten hopped out of the basket and started running toward the bird's tree. Desperately, Bugsy made a grab for it. "Come back. You don't know how dangerous it is in the jungle."

However, the kitten eluded his grasp. After darting out of his reach, it stopped and stared back at him.

"Look at what I have for you." Bugsy unwrapped the meat.

The kitten paced back and forth, eying the meat hungrily. But no matter how much the boy coaxed, it stayed where it was.

"Come back," Bugsy begged. "Please come back."

Still the kitten hesitated.

"You'll get hurt." Bugsy took a step toward the kitten. Instantly it leaped into the bushes. Calling to the kitten, he followed it into the bushes, but though he searched all around, he did not find it. Sadly, he returned to the basket, expecting the other kitten to be gone too.

He was surprised to see it calmly eating the still unwrapped meat. Gratefully, Bugsy picked up the lid again. "I guess you want love more than freedom." And he placed the lid over his remaining pet and took it to his hut, where he was never lonely again.

He cared for the kitten so that it grew into a fine, sleek animal quite happy with its way of living. And that was the first cat.

However, the other kitten had to fight for its survival. As a result, it grew as wild and deadly as the jungle it had chosen. In fact, it kept growing in size until it was very large. Then, roaming among the trees, it killed at will, terrifying all the other creatures, including humans. And that was how the first tiger came to be.

Face

Since shame was frequently used to make someone conform, it made Chinese sensitive about what others thought of them. In another words, it was important to have "face."

Most of the Chinese men who worked in America would be dreaming of the days when they could retire back in China. The ones who returned home rich built mansions for themselves and acquired great "face." "The Rat in the Wall" is a warning against taking too much pride in wealth.

There is also an old Chinese proverb, "The nail that sticks out gets hammered." It had special meaning in America, where it was often dangerous to call attention to one's self. At one time, for instance, Chinese were not allowed to testify in court. As a result, certain white hoodlums murdered Chinese with impunity; for, unless another white happened to witness the crime, there was no one to give testimony. A girl who ignores the warning to be unobtrusive almost comes to grief in "The Fatal Flower."

The final tale in this section has a bit of fun with a figure who, by centuries of tradition, has a large amount of face: the teacher. Such a man would have played an even more important role in the lives of Chinese Americans. Scholars both here and in China would write and read letters for the illiterate as well as perform other functions.

The more important the character, the more amusement a comical tale provides. A good deal of Chinese humor concerns social roles, the laughter being caused by another person's ignorance of the proper thing to do or say. However, "The Teacher's Underwear" places a man of great learning on the horns of a dilemma that any Chinese would understand: Should he lose face for being immodest or for appearing dishonest?

The
Rat
in
the
Wall

Once there was a boy named Smokey whose father, Increase, became rich—partly through hard work and partly through luck.

Smokey's family had been farmers slogging around in the mud for ten generations. Now, Increase acted as if he had never stepped in manure. He wanted everyone to bow and call him Master. Worst of all, he decided that all their former neighbors were no longer good enough for someone of their station; so Increase ordered his family not to talk to their neighbors.

He hired lots of servants, ordered precious antiques and paintings and even real four-poster beds. Soon their old house was too small for all their possessions.

"A superior man has to live in a superior house," Increase announced. "If you live like common folk, you get treated as if you're common."

To make room for his new house, he bought the houses on either side and had them torn down. Then he brought in work crews to build a fine new mansion for his family.

Unfortunately, Increase thought everyone was out to cheat him. He would look at a window and tell the carpenters they had made it smaller than he had ordered. Or he would claim a post was the wrong color. Much to Smokey's embarrassment, he found a hundred and one reasons to deduct money from the workers' pay.

When the house was finally finished, the family moved in with a grand display. Hundreds of firecrackers were set off, until the street was ankle deep in red paper.

That very night, though, as Increase settled down in his luxurious bed, he thought that he heard someone rap on his bedroom door.

Knock, knock, knock.

"Come in," he called.

When no one answered, Increase irritably got out of bed and yanked the door open, but there was no one in the hallway. He had no sooner climbed back into bed when he heard the tapping again.

Knock, knock, knock.

This time, though, he listened more closely.

Puzzled, he looked at his wife. "It's coming from the wall, not the door."

Too scared to investigate himself, Increase bellowed for his servants. When they stumbled sleepily into the master bedroom, he commanded them to search the room, but they found nothing.

Annoyed, Increase dismissed them. "It must be a rat."

Just as he and his wife lay back down in their great four-poster, the noise came even louder from within the wall.

KNOCK, KNOCK, KNOCK.

"It sounds like a giant rat!" he said, jumping out of bed.

Again, Increase summoned his servants. This time, they dragged the bed and large wardrobe away from the walls, and when they couldn't find the rat's hole, they began to inspect the rest of the mansion.

Knock, knock, knock.

The knocking continued all that night, but there were no signs of a rat.

Across the street, one of Smokey's friends had heard the knocking, too. Her name was Ruby, and, worried about Smokey, she had climbed up on to the roof to find out what was happening, but she could only hear the servants searching.

Every night, someone knocked at a door where there was no door. *Knock, knock, knock.* First it was every hour. *Knock, knock, knock.* And then it was just steady all night. *Knock, knock, knock.*

Worse things began to torment Smokey's family. Rice was burned, then one by one the family got sick. Despite all that, Increase refused to believe anything was wrong. "A little bad luck balances all the good luck we've had," he said.

Finally, a maid, too, fell sick and died. Frightened and exhausted from lack of sleep, all the servants quit. As his father stood cursing them, Smokey bowed to him. "Perhaps we should leave too until the noises stop."

His father was furious at being crossed. "Coward, letting a little rat chase you out. Go on, then." And he jerked the gates open himself and contemptuously shooed his wife and son outside. "You can be the laughingstock of the village, but not me."

Smokey's mother tugged at his arm. "We'll go across the street." So, gathering their courage, they crossed the street and knocked at Ruby's gate.

When Ruby's father saw who it was, his smile changed to a frown. "What is it now? Are you going to raise the rent on our fields?"

With a bow, Smokey humbly asked for shelter. Ruby's father scowled, but before he could say anything, Ruby began whispering urgently in his ear. "Well," he grumbled, "I guess our quarrel isn't really with you." And he let them in.

In the meantime, Increase had armed himself with a big antique cutlass he had bought to decorate his mansion. With the sword in one hand and a lantern in the other, he sat on his big four-poster bed and waited.

At sunset, a storm came. The rain lashed the streets so that no one dared to go outside; and the lightning flashed and the thunder clapped so loudly, it sounded as if the village had fallen inside a giant drum.

At the same time that it had happened every night, the knocking began.

KNOCK, KNOCK, KNOCK.

They heard it all over the village, because the knocking boomed louder even than the thunder.

"Come in, Mister Rat," Increase called.

KNOCK, KNOCK, KNOCK.

Increase set the lantern down and stood up. "I said come in!"

KNOCK, KNOCK, KNOCK.

"What are you scared of?" He shook his big sword. "Come in."

And the rat came in. But the monster in the wall was only part rat. Though it had a rat's body, it had a man's head.

The next instant a gust of wind blew out Increase's lantern; and as the lightning faded from the sky, the room became as black as an ink stick, except for a pair of eyes—red eyes, eyes like two spots of blood, eyes that burned. Slowly the eyes crept toward him.

"Never mind." Increase tried to head for the door to the hallway, but he got confused in the dark and missed it. When he felt only the wall, he whirled around. The eyes were even closer.

"Stand back." Increase began swinging his sword back and forth recklessly.

The monster rat only slunk nearer—so near that Increase could see the yellow pupils slitting the red eyes. In fact, so near he could see his own terrified reflection, trapped within the fiery eyes.

"Go away. Go 'way, goway, goway." Increase pressed against the wall for protection. To his horror, what had been wood and plaster became like rice paper. He fell right through the wall; and as he fell, he heard a door slam shut one last time.

Even through the noise of the storm, the neighbors heard him shriek. And then there was silence.

Though Ruby tried to stop him, Smokey got a lantern and went to check on his father. As thunder boomed once more overhead and the rain whipped at his face, he crossed the street and entered the dark courtyard. Room by room, he searched the dreadful mansion, but there was no sign of his father.

Smokey and his mother decided to tear down the mansion before it brought misfortune to anyone else. So Smokey went into town to hire some workers, because he knew no one in the village would go near the house. Armed with hammers and crowbars and shovels, they were led back to the the mansion and set to tearing it down. As the plaster fell in chunks at their feet, they found all sorts of bad luck charms painted on the beams of the house. The builders had put them there because of the harsh way they had been treated.[*]

Realizing he was dealing with magic, Smokey sought out the workmen. After apologizing to them for the sake of his father, Smokey paid them what they should have gotten.

When Smokey returned to the mansion, they all heard the sound of a door slamming from within the master bedroom. Rushing inside, they found Smokey's father sitting on the four-poster bed.

When they asked him where he had been, Increase shivered. "I was inside the walls, and it was very, very dark."

They tore down the mansion and built a new one— and this time they made a point of treating the builders fairly. When the mansion was ready, they moved inside.

After that, Smokey's father no longer put on airs, and instead he acted like a regular neighbor. But if someone knocked at the gates in the evening, he still almost jumped through the ceiling.

[*] It was once a common belief among Chinese that carpenters and bricklayers would take their revenge in such a way if they had not been treated right.

The
Fatal
Flower

Long ago in a faraway kingdom there was a girl called Gem who hated the way she looked. She was so ashamed that she refused to leave the house. Instead, she would stand in her little courtyard and peek through the gates at the other girls as they passed by in the village lane. "What pretty eyes she has," she would sigh. "Why can't I have eyes like that?" Or she would stare enviously at someone else. "Look at how graceful she is. Why can't I walk like that?"

Her exasperated mother would tell her that she looked fine. "You should go outside. You've got two eyes and a nose and a mouth all in the right place. Why do you have to complain all the time?"

"Because other girls have their eyes, noses, and mouths arranged much better than me," Gem insisted. "I'm so repulsive that they'll just laugh."

"It's different flowers for different eyes," her mother said. Though her mother coaxed and scolded, Gem remained inside trying to make herself beautiful.

From herbs her family gathered for her, she tried to make all sorts of pills, lotions, and ointments. Some were to make her skin smooth as silk. Others were to make her hair shiny and full. Whichever one she tried, she was always disappointed; and the smells from all her brews almost drove her family from the house. Eyes watering from the smoke and holding his nose against the stench, her father found her by the stove getting ready to throw out her latest failure. "I can't stand it anymore. They say there's a wise woman who has the power to change things. Maybe she can make you into what you want to be. Follow the river to the hill."

By now, Gem was desperate enough to try anything. The next morning before sunrise, she sneaked out with a piece of cloth wrapped around her head as a veil.

Keeping to the high riverbank, she followed the wide muddy river until she reached the hill. The wise woman's hut sat upon the top surrounded by terraced fields where herbs grew in neat, well-tended rows. Harvested herbs and flowers sat drying on the hut's roof or were hanging inside from the ceiling, so the hill smelled like a dusty garden of flowers.

Outside the little hut was a woman with black skin. She was winnowing rice—separating the harvested grains from the chaff and bits of straw. She would lay out handfuls of the harvest on a big, flat, round tray woven from bamboo and toss the contents into the air. The grain, still in its brown hulls, would rattle down while the breeze would blow the chaff and straw away.

Kneeling before the wise woman, Gem bowed. "I look like a monster, but I hear you have the power to change me into someone beautiful."

The wise woman calmly poured the winnowed rice into a basket. "First, let's see what I have to work with."

"You've been warned." Trembling, Gem unwrapped her veil. "Just look at me. I'm too gruesome to live."

The wise woman put another handful of harvested grain upon the tray. With a powerful jerk of her arms, she tossed it up into the air. Once again, the brown rice pattered down upon the tray like hard drops of rain. "Rice is ugly, but it fills the belly." Then she nodded to the chaff and bits of straw that shone like flakes of gold as they whirled around in the breeze. "While that fluff is pretty but useless."

Gem touched her forehead against the dirt, pleading with the wise woman to help her. With a sigh, the wise woman put her tray down and patted Gem on the shoulder. "Deep in the mountains there once lived a king and his daughter. The king was also a powerful wizard, and his daughter was almost as magical. When she died, she changed into a creeper with thin vines from which grow tiny yellow flowers like five-pointed stars. If your heart is set upon becoming beautiful, you must bring me a flower from that vine and I will grant your wish."

So Gem traveled beside the river until it had narrowed into a cold, steely blue ribbon and the land had slanted upward into steeper and steeper hills. Though she looked everywhere, she saw nothing. Just as she was about to turn back in discouragement, she heard a voice. "Why are you wearing that veil?"

She looked all around, but she saw no one.

"Are you deaf?" the voice repeated from overhead.

Leaning her head back, she saw a little woman perched on the branch of a tree. She wore an embroidered blouse and skirt, and Gem could see a pair of bird's claws peeking out from the dress as the strange little woman clung to a tree branch.

The little woman leaned her head to one side like a bird and studied Gem. "What's wrong?"

"Everything," the girl said, and explained her quest. "Do you know where the flowers grow?"

The little woman folded her arms smugly. "I certainly do."

Gem clung to the trunk of the tree. "Oh, please tell me."

The little woman leaned down and felt the veil. "First, you must bring me a piece of cloth as long as the river."

Gem thought long and hard while the bird-woman watched expectantly. Finally, Gem broke off a straight twig from a nearby branch. With a sharp rock, she made an elaborate show of marking the stick into ten equal units. Then she presented her homemade ruler to the bird-woman. "First, you must tell me the exact length of the river."

The bird-woman waved the ruler in annoyance. "I can't measure the whole river."

"Then I can't make a cloth as long as it. But," Gem said, and unwound her veil, "until you can measure the river, why don't you keep this as a sample gift?"

The bird-woman took the cloth, drawing it back and forth in her hands as she stared at Gem. "If I were a human, I'd be more ashamed of my fat, sloppy feet than my face."

Gem glanced at the woman's great, ugly claws but said only, "Where are the flowers?"

The bird-woman wrapped the cloth around her shoulders. "I'll show you." Leaping lightly to the ground, she began to hop along like a bird. Gem followed her among the trees until they came to a shadowy place where red pine trees grew in a circle. Though the scent of the pine was thick, Gem could smell another sweet fragrance that she could not name.

And in the center of the clearing was a tree about Gem's height around which grew a tangle of slender vines without any roots. Tiny yellow flowers rose from the tips of the vines like constellations of stars.

Excited, Gem was going to pluck handfuls of the flower but the bird-woman stopped her. "If I can have only a sample cloth, you can take only a sample flower."

Gem tried to hide her disappointment, because the flowers were so small. "Well," she sighed, "one flower will have to do." Carefully, she selected the largest of the flowers. Tucking it away safely in a sleeve, Gem reached the wise woman late in the afternoon.

"Now, please keep your promise," Gem said triumphantly.

The wise woman took the tiny stalk between her fingers. "Remember. Beauty does not always bring happiness. Do you still wish it?"

"With all my heart."

"To my mind, a girl who is clever enough to find the flower does not need to be beautiful too." The wise woman shrugged. "But so be it. Fetch me some water from the well."

Gem found a bucket and brought the water as the wise woman had asked. In the meantime, the wise woman had started a fire beneath a small stove. At the wise woman's directions, the eager girl filled a pot with water and placed it upon the top of the stove.

Then, murmuring a spell, the wise woman began to twirl the flower between her palms, faster and faster, harder and harder, until she squeezed the juice from the flower. Instantly, the hut was filled with a sweet scent that overpowered all the other fragrances. When she had wrung out the last drop, she threw the flower itself into the hole beneath the stove where the fire burned. The crushed flower disappeared in a flash of light.

Under the wise woman's watchful eye, Gem kept feeding the fire until the whole pot had almost boiled away. Carefully pouring the remaining contents into a small jar, the wise woman handed it to Gem.

"Wash your face with the first drop," the wise woman instructed. "Rub any warts and moles with the second. Swallow the third."

As the sun set, Gem skipped home clutching the jar to her chest. People turned to stare at the stranger, because no one but her own family had ever seen her. Soon, Gem said to herself, they will all be wishing they could be me.

She burst into her home, holding the jar triumphantly in the air. "I found the wise woman," she told her astounded family.

With elaborate caution, Gem poured the first drop onto her palm and washed her cheeks. Though it was only a drop, the fluid kept spreading magically until her whole face felt cool and tingly.

The second drop she massaged onto any bumps on her face, and wherever she touched, the spot burned with a pleasant warmth.

Then, raising the jar and closing her eyes, she drank the third drop. "Ai yah. Ai yah," she murmured.

"Are you feeling sick?" her mother asked anxiously.

"No." Gem hugged herself. "At least I don't think so." She gave a shiver. "But I feel as though there's lightning bouncing around inside. And each bit of lightning is tiny as an ant and they're all racing around under my skin. What kind of evil trick has the wise woman played on me?"

Terrified, Gem put her hands to her face and began to cry.

"Quick," her worried mother said. "We'll go to a doctor." The mother grabbed her wrists and tried to pull Gem toward the door.

As her mother tugged at her, Gem was forced to lower her hands. When the mother saw her daughter, she stopped in mid step.

"How terrible is it?" Gem asked. When her mother could only gape, Gem turned to her father. "Am I even more hideous?" When he only stared too, she begged her brothers to tell her, but they were as stunned as their parents.

Desperately Gem flung some water into a bowl and stared down, waiting for the water to calm down enough so she could see her reflection. She blinked when she saw the beautiful stranger gazing up at her. The stranger's face had eyebrows like the leaf of the willow, eyes like kernels of apricots, a mouth like a cherry, a face shaped like a melon seed.

Cautiously, hardly daring to believe, she raised a hand to touch her face. Upon the surface of the water, the lovely stranger also raised a delicate hand.

"It worked," she said. "It worked!"

Word of her beauty quickly spread through the countryside, for there was no one as lovely as she.

About that time, though, the king of the land fell sick with a terrible fever that burned through his body like flames through an old log. Hurriedly his doctors examined him and, after a lengthy consultation among themselves, went to his heir, the prince. "Everyone has the elements of Yin and Yang. His Highness burns because he has too much fiery Yang and must be cooled with Yin. Because his illness is so severe, it must be quickly countered with a powerful dose."

"What are you waiting for?" the prince demanded. "Do it!"

The doctors bowed deeply, and their chief hardly dared to look up at the angry prince. "We regret to inform you that Yin is most concentrated in the heart of a beautiful girl. We must cut it out."

The prince paled. "Is there no other way?"

The chief doctor apologized and said. "It would take too long to gather it from other sources. He must have a broth made from such a heart as soon as possible, or His Highness will surely die."

The prince took a breath and then nodded. "So be it." That very night he sent men racing from the palace across the kingdom to fetch back the most beautiful girls.

In her village, Gem woke to the frightened cries and the wailing. Her sleepy father staggered into the lane to find out what was happening. Hastily he scurried back, wide-eyed with the news. "Everyone with a pretty daughter is telling the king's men to come here for you. They want to cut out your heart."

"Quickly. Go hide in the hills," her mother ordered her daughter. "We'll put up a fuss and distract them for as long as we can."

Gem slid out of the courtyard gate and darted away from the lights by the village gates. Moving a cart against the village walls, she managed to climb to the top of a wall. To her dismay, she saw men with torches ringing the village.

She dropped back down within the village and tried to hide, but the other villagers, fearing for the lives of their own daughters, pointed at Gem and called to the king's men. Not knowing where else to go, she stumbled into the temple of the goddess of mercy. As she heard the mob coming toward her, she collapsed in despair.

The next instant there was a flash of light and the wise woman was standing there with her arms folded in front of her. With a cry, Gem crawled on her hands and knees toward the wise woman. "Save me. This cursed beauty will be my death."

The wise woman looked down at her sternly. "Make up your mind. Are you too beautiful or too ugly to live?"

However, as the terrified girl begged for help, the wise woman's expression softened. From her sleeve, she produced another small jar. "I thought you might be needing this, so I saved the last three drops. Use them as before."

Shaking with fright, Gem took the jar from the wise woman, who disappeared just as quickly as she had come. Hastily Gem rubbed one drop on her face, dotted her face with the second, and swallowed the third.

As the mob burst into the temple, they found Gem cowering upon the floor of the temple. Sure that they had found the most beautiful girl, they yanked her to her feet; but when they saw her, they became angry. "She's just an ordinary girl," their captain said. "They've just been playing a trick on us."

And kicking and slapping the villagers who had led them there, the soldiers left Gem alone in the temple.

As it turned out, the king's fever broke that night and he recovered. And when he was well and heard what had almost happened, he dismissed all his old doctors and hired new ones.

As for Gem, she found her looks were adequate for her needs.

The
Teacher's
Underwear

There once was a teacher called Patience. Year after year, he took the government tests that would have let him become an official. Unfortunately, he was rather forgetful, so year after year he always flunked. However, he was so determined that he still sat for the exams, though he was now an old man.

In order to eat, he taught school in a small village in the hills within a side room of the temple dedicated to the clan's ancestors. Because he did not earn very much, he had only one robe and one pair of underpants. As he said to himself, It's not what you wear, it's what you know.

One school holiday he strung up a clothesline in his room and washed his one pair of underpants. Then he got out his favorite book of wise sayings and began to leaf through it. As the water dripped down like raindrops, he happened to read, "Pride harvests disaster; humility gathers the reward."

He was just settling back to meditate upon the proverb when someone knocked. Throwing on his only robe, he went outside to the schoolroom and opened its door.

It was one of his students, Evergreen, a son of the richest man in the village. His pupil bowed in formal politeness. "Master, my older brother is getting married today. We have the pigs and the musicians, but we lack a man of learning—someone who can grace us with his wisdom at the banquet. Will you come?"

Thinking of the wedding feast, Patience's belly began to grumble. He would have loved to go and eat his fill for once; but he thought of his one pair of underpants dripping water in the back room.

His pride counted more than his belly, so he heaved a big sigh. "I would love to go," he said, "but I have a lot of papers to grade."

However, it wasn't long before Evergreen returned. His family was used to getting its way in the clan. Since the clan elders were already gathered at the house for the wedding, the rich man had begged them to excuse Patience from schoolwork. As part of the atmosphere of goodwill, the elders had quickly agreed and summoned Patience to the wedding.

Patience could not give the real reason he could not go: that he had just washed his only pair of underpants. So he went up to the wedding with nothing on underneath his long scholar's robe.

The rich man himself gave Patience a bowl of wine, and in no time Patience became drunk. When his host asked him to recite some poetry for the happy occasion, Patience got his poems all muddled and wound up reciting most of a poem about fighting the Huns. However, the clan liked their absentminded scholar and thanked him anyway.

Now, as the party went on, people began the usual teasing and joking. Eventually Evergreen and his schoolmates decided to play their own trick. Among the many wedding presents was a jade bracelet. Taking it, they slipped out of the house and hid it in an empty bird's nest in a nearby tree.

A servant soon noticed that it was missing and told the rich man that the bracelet had been stolen. Immediately, one of the clan elders rose and announced that everyone there must be searched and the guilty culprit caught.

Off to one side, Evergreen and the others had trouble stifling their laughter; and they nudged one another with their elbows at how well their prank was going. Their teacher, however, tugged at his wispy little beard, suffering agonies of embarrassment. If he allowed them to search him, the whole village would know that he wasn't wearing any underwear.

When the guests began to line up, Patience made

sure he was at the end of the line. He hoped that they would find the bracelet before it became his turn. As he watched each man ahead of him being searched, Patience became more and more nervous. By the time it was his turn, he had begun to panic.

He flapped his hands at the searchers, motioning for them to stay away. "I am a gentleman and a scholar. I can't let you examine me."

The rich man and the clan elders looked at him sternly. "Each of us was inspected. There's no shame, unless . . ."

"No, I can't, I can't," Patience insisted wildly.

Everyone there could see how agitated Patience was, and one old gossip mistook his nervousness for a guilty conscience. "He must be the thief," the gossip said out loud.

Patience overheard him, as he was meant to do. Blushing a furious red, he shoved his way through the crowd and scampered out of the house, muttering that he simply couldn't let them search him.

"Thief! Thief!" everyone shouted, and rushed after him.

With a mob at his heels, Patience stumbled back to his rooms. Finding his underpants dry, he hurriedly snatched them from the line and put them on. As the mob began to pound at his door, he opened it and regarded them with all the dignity he could muster under the circumstances.

"Very well. Since you are so set on searching me, go ahead."

They inspected the schoolteacher and then the rooms but they found nothing. However, the damage had been done. The gossips figured that he had stashed the bracelet somewhere during his desperate flight from the party.

For their part, Evergreen and the other boys were so shocked at the near riot their simple prank had caused, they were now too afraid to tell people what had really happened.

As a result, the village became convinced that Patience must be dishonest. The next day none of his pupils showed up for school, because no family wanted a thief teaching their children.

During the next few weeks, Patience had to sneak into town to sell his beloved books. As he parted with the book of wise sayings, he thought again about the proverb he had read on that fateful wedding day: "Pride harvests disaster; humility gathers the reward."

He looked around the bookstore at his much-loved books scattered around the shelves. "How true, how true," he muttered. Then he took his cash and left without another word.

For months, he ignored the clan's suspicious stares. He had hoped he could wait until people came to their senses, but they didn't, and he went through all of his money. After he had eaten the last of his rice, he waited till evening when everyone else was asleep. Then he picked up a rice bowl and found a stick to beat off dogs. Closing his school for the last time, Patience stole out of the village.

The old man roamed from town to town, but he did not beg. Rather he "tutored" by reciting poems, essays, history, and whatever else he could remember from his vanished library. He would stand in the square among the vegetable and meat stalls, and while others sold cabbages and slabs of pork, he sold "pearls of wisdom."

At night, the stars were his ceiling and the ground was his bed. After several years, his robe grew quite ragged and his hair dirty and straggly.

One day he wound up in a strange town, where he took up a position among the stalls. Holding out his bowl to passersby, he began to quote from memory.

Most people mistook him for another beggar and ignored his bowl, but one young man stopped and stared, as happened sometimes. Years of suffering and humiliation had only made Patience's memory worse, and he mixed up his poems so much now that the rhythm and rhyme and meaning were a poetical stew.

"What terrible thing has forced a man of your learning to beg for a living?" the young man asked.

After years of living on the road, Patience's own life now seemed like a story to him, so he began to recite, "Learn from my example, young master: Even pride has its place." And Patience told about washing his one pair of underpants, the disastrous wedding party, and the bracelet that vanished.

As it turned out, the young man was Evergreen himself. So he bowed now to his old teacher. "Forgive me, Master, for not recognizing you." Evergreen kept his head down. "Master, we wondered what happened when you left in the middle of the night."

Patience sighed. "The village probably thought I got the bracelet from where I hid it and sold it. But if I were a thief, would I be living like this?"

Shamefaced, Evergreen shook his head. "I know where the bracelet is. I helped to take it and hide it. At first, we were afraid to confess because of all the uproar. And by the time we had worked up the nerve, you had vanished. It's haunted us ever since. Thank Heaven that I've found you."

Patience gripped Evergreen's arm, hardly daring to believe his ears. "Let's go back and return the bracelet."

Evergreen wanted to take Patience to a barber first and buy him a new set of clothes, but Patience had only one thought: He wanted to clear his name. They set out that very hour for the village, reaching it in the late afternoon. Everyone stared at the wild-looking old beggar with Evergreen, and they followed them as the young man guided Patience to the tree. "There it is. All of us were too ashamed to touch it all these years."

They returned the bracelet to the rich man, and Evergreen explained all about the prank. When his friends were summoned, they supported his story.

"We owe you a great apology," the elders confessed to Patience. "What can we do for you?"

Patience groomed himself clumsily with his hands. "I would like back my school."

"Done."

"And a new robe."

"Done."

"And"—Patience smiled sheepishly—"because prudence is also a virtue, I would like two pairs of underpants."

He could have had much more from the embarrassed clan. "But you're a scholar," they protested. "A scholar without books is like a dragon without its teeth."

So they bought back Patience's old library and replaced the books that they couldn't find.

Reunited with his beloved books and wearing his new clothes, Patience reopened his school's doors. Shamefaced families brought their children to him until his school was quite full. And for the rest of his days, he was a busy man. Nor did he ever have to do his laundry again. As a penance, the clan elders ordered the pranksters to take turns washing their victim's underwear.

Beyond the Grave

It's difficult to emphasize just how important it was to obey a parent's wishes, but it was enough to compel obedient sons to risk a long, dangerous ocean voyage as well as all the perils of America. Nor did obligations end with death. As in "The Magical Horse," a son was expected to honor his parents' wishes even though they had passed on.

Then, too, the wishes of the dead were important in another way for Chinese Americans. If anything happened to a guest of the Golden Mountain, his friends and family eventually shipped his bones home to rest finally in the soil of home. Reburial was important, no matter what the cost. Letting greed obstruct a last wish could be as fatal as it was for the collector in "Eyes of Jade."

The final story, "The Ghostly Rhyme," is a humorous tale about a forgetful ghost. I like to think it's a parable for anyone trying to voice the Chinese American experience, for that experience is like a poem whose rhymes are still unfinished.

The
Magical
Horse

Many years ago there lived a wonderful painter. No one could paint animals as he could. Ducks flew from his paintings. Monkeys leaped from trees. Tigers bounded.

Despite his skill, no one would buy his paintings because he mixed his paints with the saliva of old men. He didn't care, because none of his own paintings satisfied him. "My hands chase what my heart admires," he would often say, "and always in vain."

As a result, he never painted the animal he loved the most: the horse. "To paint a horse, I must paint beauty and nobility itself, but I am merely a clumsy dabbler whose paintings have no spirit."

He put it off for years, trying to paint instead what he called the lesser animals and the lesser virtues. One day he looked in the mirror and saw the reflection of an old man. With a shock, he realized that he did not have to collect anyone else's spit anymore. He could use his own.

He had a boy named Sunny, his only relation, who had been born late in his life before his wife had died. He called Sunny in now and announced his decision. "I have waited all these years for my skill to match my love; and now I have almost run out of time. Though I am still a hopeless bungler, today I shall begin my painting of a horse."

It was not to be any horse, though, but a horse that could run a thousand miles without growing tired. Day after day he sketched, until his studies covered the room in layers. And day by day, he and Sunny grew poorer. They had to sell everything—all his paintings and then their furniture and even the house.

Still he kept on, until one day he announced he was ready to paint a thousand-mile horse. Standing before the long, narrow canvas, he squatted down as if he were actually on a saddle. He forgot about the cold and his hunger and his many years, and his brush flew. Sunny begged him to rest, but the painter ignored his son as he painted a snow-white mare that seemed almost to fly across the plains. At the end of the day, the painter set his brush down and announced that he was nearly done.

Sunny stared in awe at his father's masterpiece. "What more could you do to the painting? Every stroke is perfect."

"It needs one thing more," the painter said, and sat down weakly. "But first swear that you won't sell this painting until it is time."

When Sunny promised, his father silently held up his arms for Sunny to lift him. "But how will I know?" Sunny asked.

"The painting will tell you." The painter looked at the magnificent horse upon the narrow rectangle and then heaved a large sigh. With that last breath, his spirit left his body and passed into the painting itself.

Sadly, Sunny lowered his father's now lifeless body onto the floor and then went begging for the money to bury his father.

"It's your father's own fault that you have no money," the neighbors said smugly.

So the faithful son had to sell himself to a farmer for the necessary money.

When he had buried his father, he moved into the farmer's barn. His one possession was the painting, which he put up on the wall. Staring up at the horse, Sunny wished that he could carry on his father's work, but he knew that he had not inherited his father's skill. "My hands can never pursue what my heart desires," Sunny said to himself. "But his memory will live as long as I do." So that first night, he begged some incense sticks from the farmer.

"It won't make the barn smell any better." The farmer laughed.

"This is for my father's spirit, which he gave to the painting," Sunny said. And the farmer was so ashamed that he provided Sunny with incense sticks.

As the boy sat with his body aching from the hard work and eating his cold rice, he gazed up at the painting. His father had caught the horse as if it were suspended upon one hoof. And as he watched, the horse's sides seemed to heave in the moonlight—as if it were breathing in the incense. On a whim, Sunny set out feed for his painted horse just as he did for the other animals.

He slept among the beasts for warmth, so he was not surprised when he felt an animal's warm breath blow on him. When a nose nudged him, he sat up irritated, intending to shove the creature away, but his hand paused in the air.

By the light of the moon, he saw a silvery horse standing over him. He looked over at the wall where the painting had been and saw that the canvas was empty. The next thing he knew, he was on the back of the horse, his hands clinging to the flying mane, the horse's hooves booming rhythmically along a road that gleamed like a silver ribbon winding up into the sky. And his sadness evaporated like rain hitting hot stones.

The next morning, when Sunny woke up, he found the feed was gone. "So it was real," Sunny said. "It wasn't a dream."

Each night after that, he would take his meal with

the magical horse; and each night he rode the marvelous beast to wherever he wanted, because even great distances melted beneath those miraculous hooves.

One evening Sunny took it into his head to see the king's palace, and they galloped up to the very walls of the great palace with its golden roof tiles.

Now the prince happened to be looking out his window and saw Sunny and the white horse flash past in the blink of an eye; and in that same blink, the prince wanted a horse just like that.

So the next morning he went to his father, the king. "I have one of everything in my collection of wonders. I have a phoenix's egg. I have the whiskers from the chin of a dragon king. But I do not have a thousand-mile horse."

"You have plenty of horses in the stable already," the king argued.

"None of them can travel as far and as fast as a thousand-mile horse," the prince insisted.

So the king, who could never say no to his son, offered six hundred pieces of silver to the person who brought him such a magical horse.

The farmer shook his head when he heard the news. "It's too bad that you don't have a real thousand-mile horse instead of a painted one."

Sunny, though, wasn't sorry at all, for if he were to sell his painting, he would miss his midnight rides.

People hunted all over for a thousand-mile horse.

The honest ones searched by day, but there was a thief who looked by night. He sneaked through the forts and looked at the cavalry chargers. He stole onto the big farms and examined all the animals. Nowhere did he find a thousand-mile horse.

Then one night as he was leaving a stable, he heard the drumming of hooves. He looked up just in time to see a boy riding a gleaming horse; and then they were gone in a single breath. However, he had time to see that the horse's tail was burned. At first he thought he was dreaming; but then in the moonlight he saw the hoofprints.

Eagerly, the thief followed the trail. It took many days, and several times he lost the tracks in all the traffic in the road, but he always managed to find them again until he reached the farm.

Hiding in a bush, he scratched his head in puzzlement. "The tracks come from there, but what is a thousand-mile horse doing in a miserable place like that?" Even so, he kept a watch on the place.

Sure enough, the magical horse appeared with the rising of the moon. In the time it took the thief to gulp, the horse and rider had vanished from sight. A while later, they reappeared, leaped over the wall, and entered the barn.

Using all his skill, the thief sneaked into the farm and entered the barn. He saw Sunny asleep among the animals, but there was no thousand-mile horse.

Suddenly the thief noticed the painting. An incense stick had burned part of the canvas near the horse's tail. He realized, then, that the horse in the painting was magical. He was just about to snatch the painting from the wall when he heard a rooster crow, and the farm began to stir. Hurriedly the thief fled.

The next day he carefully asked questions around the neighborhood before he visited the farm. "I have always wanted a painting by that master. I'll give you eighty cash," the thief offered.

His price made the farmer's jaw drop open. "Sell it," he urged Sunny.

However, Sunny refused. "A promise is a promise."

"That's what I get for trying to be honest," the thief muttered. He went as far as his bush and dropped out of sight to wait until everyone had gone to the fields. Then he sneaked back into the barn and stole the painting.

He hid in an abandoned shack until nightfall and then hung up the painting of the thousand-mile horse. He planned to ride the horse to the palace that very night.

When the moon shone through the doorway of the shack, the horse reappeared, but he seemed puzzled to see the thief and not the painter's son. When the thief grasped the horse's bridle, the beast reared and kicked, and it was all the thief could do to keep out of the way of the flailing hooves.

"Stop that," he ordered the horse, "or I'll burn the painting tomorrow morning."

The next instant, the horse was still, trembling where it stood. Hardly daring to believe his luck, the thief took down the now-empty scroll and led the creature outside.

Rolling up the scroll, the thief scrambled onto the magical horse's back. "Take me to the king's palace," he commanded.

The horse thundered off. Trees flashed by in the wink of an eye. The wind of their passage tore the scroll from the thief's hand. "Stop. Go back," the thief cried.

The horse only galloped faster, and the world— houses and hills, streams and valleys—whizzed by in a blur. If I fall off now, the thief thought, I'll break every bone in my body. With that in mind, the desperate thief grabbed the whipping mane in both hands and held on for dear life.

When the horse finally slowed down, the thief saw that they were not at the king's palace but in some garden where rocks rose upward like mountains from pools fashioned like miniature seas.

Ahead of them, through the moonlit trees, he saw a magnificent mansion. Everything seemed hushed and still. Even his mount's hooves hardly made a sound.

He rubbed his hands gleefully. "This horse is worth more than six hundred pieces of silver. I can ride it to faraway places to loot and be back home the very same night so no one could ever suspect me. Whatever my heart wants, my hands can take."

Jumping off the horse, he tied it to a bush and patted its neck. "I'm going to keep you for myself." And he sneaked inside the mansion.

Now Sunny had been terribly upset when he found the painting missing. He had searched all over the farm, and when he could find no trace of it, he had run away to hunt for it in the countryside. He looked everywhere until he finally lay down, exhausted, and fell asleep.

When he first felt the warm breath blowing at his ear, he thought he was dreaming, but when he felt the muzzle nudging him, he sat up joyfully and saw the magical white horse. It had managed to pull itself free. Climbing onto the magical creature's back, he let himself be carried to a tree not very far from the bush where the thief had hidden. In the branches where it had been blown, he found the scroll.

Once the scroll was safely rolled up and tucked under his arm, he told the horse to take him back to the farm. Instead, the horse took him in the opposite direction until they saw the king's palace in the distance. The royal roof was a gleaming red dot when the sun rose. Immediately, Sunny plopped down on the road as the horse disappeared from the road. Hurriedly he unrolled the scroll to see that the horse had reappeared once again in the painting.

Sorrowfully, Sunny remembered his father's words then. He knew that this was the sign that he should sell the painting now.

It took most of the morning to reach the palace itself. When he reached the gates, he found the whole place in an uproar because someone had vandalized a very rare painting.

At first, the gatekeeper didn't want to admit the ragged boy who claimed to have a thousand-mile horse, but since the gatekeeper was under orders to admit anyone who might satisfy the prince's whim, he eventually let Sunny in.

Sunny was passed from one reluctant servant to another until he was led into the throne room, where the king and prince were both examining the ruined painting.

"If this is the work of a vandal," the prince observed, "then it's a very talented vandal. This thief is lifelike."

The king was tugging at his beard. "It is not the thief's talent but his intentions that worry me. If someone could get past all my guards to do this, he could get into my very bedroom to kill me."

As Sunny waited to be introduced to the king, he looked up at the long scroll. His father, he thought, had painted far better, but it was a good old-fashioned landscape of a mansion nestled within an elaborate garden.

The king turned to his counselors and his generals. "Find out who this is, and find out at once." And he stepped back to point at one corner of the painting.

There, near a bush in the garden, was the thief. His mouth was open and his hands were pressed flat as if he were calling for help from the other side of a window.

"That's the man who tried to buy my painted horse," Sunny gasped.

All eyes turned to Sunny, much to his discomfort. "Do you know this man?" the king demanded.

So Sunny told everything he knew—from his father's painting of the horse to its loss and recovery.

"Let me see the painting," the king commanded.

When the scroll was unrolled, his eyes gleamed appreciatively. "Your father was truly a master. I can believe that this painting comes to life. The horse almost seems to be breathing right now before my very eyes." He looked back at the picture of the thief. "And if a painted horse can come to life, then perhaps a live thief can become a painting."

So the king ordered Sunny's painting to be hung up in the garden, and that evening everyone gathered to watch. As the first rays of moonlight touched the painting, the magical horse leaped to the ground, where it stood, stamping its hooves.

First the king and then his son took a quick canter and pronounced themselves satisfied that this was indeed a thousand-mile horse. They not only gave Sunny a large sum of money but invited him to live in the palace. So, after buying his freedom, Sunny settled down to a comfortable life.

And whenever the prince lacked the time or the desire for a gallop, he would send the horse to the painter's son, and Sunny would once again take long rides in the moonlight.

Eyes
of
Jade

Once there was a man who collected jade. He dreamed and schemed of owning the largest collection of jade in the empire—larger even than the emperor's.

One day a man approached him politely on the street and held up a small bundle on his palm. "I understand that you are a great collector. May we go inside? I found a few old stones. I don't think they're worth much, but would you mind looking at them?"

The collector looked at the man's gnarled, dirty fingers and ragged clothes. Suspecting he was a robber, the collector shook his head suspiciously. "I'm in a hurry. Show them to me now or not at all."

Nervously, the man glanced all around; but they were alone in the street, so he untied the knot that held the ragged bundle together. Peeling away the rag, he revealed a round amulet of the sort that Chinese

177

long ago used to put on the belly of the dead—though that custom was no longer practiced.

"I'm a smith by trade," the man explained. "I know about iron and bronze. I don't know the first thing about precious stones."

"There isn't much call for this sort of thing nowadays, but I collect curiosities too," the collector said. He bargained with the smith, and when they settled on a price that was far less than the piece was worth, the collector congratulated himself on his cleverness.

The next week the smith again approached him— this time with an old piece of tan jade that he said he had just found. It was in the shape of a tooth, and long ago people used it to protect the teeth of a corpse.

The collector bought that one also, but when the smith sought him out a week later with another antique piece, the collector suspected that the smith had found some ancient tomb and was stealing things from it at night.

Now the collector didn't care how he got the jade; but he was curious. "Are you robbing some grave?" he asked quietly.

The smith paled. "No. It's all quite honest."

With a thin smile, the collector threatened to go to the officials and report the smith unless he told him the truth.

"I thought I could trust you," the man said tearfully.

"I don't buy just the jade, but its story as well," the

collector said. "I have to know."

"I mustn't tell," the man insisted.

The collector threatened and coaxed until the smith reluctantly admitted that the jade had all belonged to his wife. "If we didn't need expensive medicines, we would never sell them," the smith admitted.

Patting him on the shoulder, the collector promised that he would tell no one else, but he must see the collection of the smith's wife. They argued for a bit more, until the smith reluctantly promised to ask his wife.

Later that evening, the smith got the collector and took him to his house, where he met the smith's wife. She was a small, sickly woman who winced as she moved and touched her stomach as if there were some sharp pain there. "Those things were in my family for generations," she explained. "The emperor himself sent us the jade as gifts, but my family fell on hard times. My husband was just trying to save me from embarrassment, for I am the last of my family; and I am afraid that I will be passing on soon."

The smith patted his wife's hand anxiously. "Don't be silly. The medicine is making you better by the day."

The collector felt ashamed for forcing that confession from the woman. "Houses rise and houses fall," he said kindly. "And if things seem bad now, they can change."

He spoke comfortingly to her and finally asked to see her collection.

The woman hesitated and then sighed. "You're a man famous for his knowledge of jade. I suppose it's only right that they should be appreciated by someone like you."

The husband proudly brought in a small wooden chest and set it before his wife, who opened it and un- wrapped the ordinary cotton cloth. All the jade was very old, and the collector wanted it. However, when he saw the last pieces of jade, he gave a gasp, for they were both of yellow jade. Oval shaped, they were carved with slits like the pupils of a cat. Long ago, people had covered the eyes of a corpse with such pieces.

"This jade is very rare."

"They aren't half bad?" the smith asked, and he wrapped them up again.

As he watched the cloth hide the jade again, the col- lector forced himself to find words. "They are priceless, exquisite."

"We sold you the lesser ones. We have no children," the woman said. "When I die, the remaining pieces shall be buried with me."

"Like a princess of old," the smith boasted.

Shaking his head, the collector went home. But all that night he could not forget the woman's collection, for it was far better than that of many famous collectors—far better even than his. Somehow, he decided, he must add it to his own.

He began to visit the smith and his wife; and the wife was pleased to talk about the prosperous days when she had been young. Gradually, as he won her trust, the wife told him her story. Her father had joined in a conspiracy against the last emperor, and as punishment, his whole line had been killed. An old nursemaid had managed to get her away with the jewelry chest and passed her off as a niece so that the woman would not be killed.

They spoke mostly about jade, though, for the woman knew almost as much as the collector. "It's silly to hold on to a bunch of stones when you could live in comfort," the collector said. "Let me buy your collection. No one will ever know you were the original owner, and there will be no danger to you."

"Where would you get enough money? But even if you could, they are mine and they will go with me into the grave." The woman clutched at her stomach. She did that more and more often, as if the medicine had only slowed her illness, not ended it.

The collector tried to argue that it wasn't right for such loveliness to disappear into the dirt, but the woman was stubborn.

The next morning, the smith found her dead with her hands wrapped around her stomach. Standing outside in frustration, the collector watched the coffin enter the smith's house. The smith's family gathered in white mourning robes and sang wailingly for her; but they would wait for a lucky day to bury her.

All that night, the collector lay on his mat and thought about what was happening. He could picture it in his mind. And all that night, it seemed as if he could hear the yellow jade whispering to him: "We are here. Free us. Free us."

At first, the collector tried to ignore the whispers; but more and more he began to resent the willful woman who wanted to take the jade back into the earth. The pieces had been freed from the dirt long ago, and had been worked so lovingly and with such skill that they should be appreciated, not hidden again. And, he told himself, they should be appreciated by someone who knew how to value such things—someone like the collector.

And so, in the darkness of his room, the collector finally began to whisper back in answer, "I will. I will."

After that, the collector haunted the corner near the house. Finally one day, he saw the coffin brought outside. Some of the mourners scattered ghost money to confuse greedy ghosts who might be around. Keeping his distance, he followed them to a cemetery on a hill where the coffin was buried, and he marked the spot where food and drink were left for the dead woman.

That evening, the collector got a shovel and sneaked out of his house. He started when he saw a pale object drift toward him. As soon as he realized it was only a ragged yellow cat, he kicked at it. "Shoo."

However, as he crept through the dark streets of the town, the cat kept a safe distance behind him, following him all the way into the cemetery.

There, paper prayers fluttered in the breeze. Scavenging animals had scattered the meat that had been laid out on the plates and knocked over the jar of wine so the dregs were trickling into the dark earth—as if the grave itself were drinking.

The collector almost ran for home; but his greed was stronger than his fear. Gripping his shovel tightly, he began to dig. At first, he scooped out the earth in small piles, but it was almost as if he could hear the jade once again whispering to him, and soon the shovel began to fly. The collector was not used to such labor, and his soft hands were soon bleeding and blistered, but he did not care.

When his shovel hit the lid, he quickly exposed the coffin. With the edge of his shovel, he pried the lid up. It rose in a protesting creak, and he hesitated, looking around. For a moment, his heart stopped when he saw a pair of golden eyes glowing in the moonlight; and then he realized it was the old yellow cat sitting on the pile of dirt he had heaped next to the grave. The cat watched him with large, unblinking eyes.

The collector told himself it had been drawn there by the offerings. "Shoo. Go on." He raised the shovel threateningly, but the cat simply sat there. Finally he reached down, found a clod of dirt, and flung it at the cat, which darted away at last.

Then the collector looked down. Though the woman lay there in a robe of white, there was no sign of the yellow jade. He searched frantically, but there were no precious jewels. The collector cursed himself for a fool. "The smith must have kept it after all."

Just as he was about to set the lid back down, the cat reappeared upon the mound, crouching on the damp, newly turned soil.

"Shoo. Go away, you pest." Glad of having a target for his anger, he reached for another lump of dirt.

The cat, though, sprang into the air, leaping over the open coffin. The startled collector heard a sigh like a dusty bellows. He looked down to see the corpse's jaw had cracked open, and her chest rose and fell as she took a breath. Slowly, the eyelids peeled back like old curtains, and her eyes shone with a golden light—like yellow jade.

Desperately the collector dropped the coffin lid. Grabbing the shovel, he tried to hammer it shut. As he banged the shovel blade against the lid's nails, the corpse gave a loud, piercing shriek.

Thump. Thump. Thump. Her fists beat at the coffin lid, and her blows were so strong that they broke the wooden planks.

As the woman sat up in her coffin, the collector

swung the shovel with all his strength. However, she was as strong in death as she had been weak in life. Catching the shovel, she wrestled it out of his hands.

Terrified, the collector scrambled out of the hole and rushed out of the cemetery. Behind him, he saw the corpse running with her white gown streaming in back of her.

The collector ran as fast as he could, but her footsteps got closer and closer. Puffing, he darted into town and up the silent streets. "Help, help," he called, and raced for his house.

He got out his keys and fumbled at the lock. Just as he got it open, he felt cold hands grab his waist. With the same supernatural strength, she lifted the shrieking man from his feet. Hugging him against her, she took him straight to the underworld. There, surrounded by the dead, he saw more jade than he had ever wanted to—forever and ever.

The
Ghostly
Rhyme

Long ago a wise man once wrote a letter to the emperor. In it, the wise man criticized an imperial minister as corrupt and gave examples as proof. However, because the official was the emperor's favorite, it was the wise man and not the minister who was punished.

The wise man was sent south, where much of the land was still jungle. At first, he settled in a town that had grown up outside the walls of a Chinese fort. There he made friends with the other exiles.

Eventually, though, he moved into the jungle itself, where he built a small thatched hut among the cinnamon trees. Near his hut a stream ran, its water still fresh and cool from the mountains.

With a little bamboo dipper he had made himself, he would fetch the water for his tea, and then, cup in hand, he would spend all day reading.

For food, he fished in the nearby stream or picked wild fruit or gathered the vegetables he grew in a small patch outside his hut. And for wine, he had the scent of the surrounding cinnamon trees, which was so thick it would make anyone drunk. But even when he was fishing or picking fruit or gardening, he would insist that he was thinking about what he read.

Once when a friend asked him why he lived in such a lonely spot, he was surprised. "But I'm not alone," he said. "My books have told me all about these hills. I have the spirits of the woods and the dragons in the water for company." He motioned to some spotted bamboo. "And it's said these are the family of an emperor; they were transformed into these plants as they mourned him."

Meditating about what he had read, he would go for walks in the shadowy pines among the hills to where the icy rivers exploded from between the sharp, craggy mountains; and he would stand there as the spray of the waterfall fell about him like rain. And at night he would stare up at the night sky and his mind would go voyaging among the stars.

When he developed a cough, his friends tried to get him to come down to the city to see a doctor, but he refused. "The smell of pine is the best medicine."

One day, he picked up a book by his favorite poet. Unfortunately, worms had gotten at the book and eaten away the outside edges of the pages. Annoyed, he opened the book to examine the damage, and his eye happened to fall upon a particular page. Most of the poems he knew by heart, but as he read the poem, he found he could not remember the last line, which was missing.

He prided himself upon his knowledge, so he sat there through the long afternoon and into the evening, trying to remember the last line. To prod his memory, he kept reciting the next to the last line over and over:

"The sun on my old garden shines . . ."

He forgot to eat and even sleep. His friends, bringing some food and books up to him, found him still inside his hut, the worm-eaten book upon his lap. He had died with a very annoyed look on his face.

Sadly, they buried him with the book; but that night as the wind shook the cinnamon and pine trees, people thought it sounded like someone sighing. And as the rain began to fall, the drops pattered down like some-one impatiently tapping a finger.

His friends saw his ghost reading the poem out loud; but he stopped just before the last line. Then, with a very irritated look on his face, the ghost disappeared. At first people were frightened, but they realized that as a ghost he was just as harmless as he had been in real life.

However, when the rainy season came, his ghost would walk out of the jungle and into town to visit his friends' houses, where he would recite his one line.

Eventually, though, he began to haunt the main street itself and speak the words in a loud voice. It didn't take long before the ghost started to wear on people's nerves. "If only he would recite something else—a limerick or a riddle or even a jingle. But it's always the same line." There were some nights when the poetical ghost kept everyone up.

They pleaded with the ghost to go away; or if he wouldn't go away, at least he could quote something else. They tried bribes and threats. He ignored them, though, as obsessed in death as he had been in life.

Reluctantly, they called in a priest to exorcise the ghost; but the ghost insisted on reading his ghostly rhyme over and over until it was the priest who finally banged his head against the wall in frustration and gave up.

At last, a poet heard about the literate ghost. Having a taste for the strange and fantastical, the poet went up to the wise man's home. Sitting down by the now ruined hut, he waited as the storm clouds rolled in overhead.

The wind rushed through the trees like someone sighing heavily. And the raindrops fell like someone tapping his finger impatiently. As the poet sat up, he saw the old man in his tattered robe with the worm-eaten book in his hand.

As he watched, the ghost began to read from the book. Now it happened that the poet liked the same writer. As the ghost spoke, the poet thought he had never heard the poem read better or more movingly.

When the ghost stopped just before the last line, the poet urged him, "Go on."

However, the ghost started to recite the poem over again, halting at the same place. "The sun on my old garden shines . . ."

"But I am gone," the poet finished. "No flesh confines."

The wind roared through the trees, and the rain fell in showers. Standing in the middle of the storm, the ghost smiled in relief and clapped his book shut. Tucking it under his arm, the ghost disappeared, and no one ever saw or heard him again.

AFTERWORD

The original stories were gathered by Jon Lee in Oakland's Chinatown as part of a WPA project in the 1930's and collected in *The Golden Mountain*.

"The Ghostly Rhyme" is the only exception. It was collected in San Francisco's Chinatown by Wolfram Eberhard and published in his article "A Study of Ghost Stories from Taiwan and San Francisco" in *Asian Folklore Series.*, Vol. 30, Number 2 (1971), pp. 1–26. I want to thank the editor, Peter Knecht, for granting permission to retell it.

For those wanting a general discussion of Chinese folk and supernatural tales, let me suggest the introduction to

Karl S. Y. Kao's *Classical Chinese Tales of the Supernatural and the Fantastic* (Bloomington, Indiana: Indiana University, 1985).
Let me also recommend the following:

The Golden Mountain: Chinese Tales Told in California, collected and translated by Jon Lee and edited by Paul Radin with notes by Wolfram Eberhard (Taipei, Taiwan: The Orient Cultural Service, 1972).

Folktales of China, edited and translated by Wolfram Eberhard (Chicago: University of Chicago Press, 1965).

Hong Kong Tale-Spinners, compiled and translated by Bertha Hensman (Hong Kong: Chinese University of Hong Kong, 1968).

More Hong Kong Tale-Spinners, compiled and translated by Bertha Hensman (Hong Kong: Chinese University of Hong Kong, 1971)